Ring of Love

Ring of Love

MARION CATTERALL

Ring of Love

ACKNOWLEDGEMNTS

To my dearest husband,
William; my two sons, David and Stephen;
and my three girls, Jennifer, Clare, and Sarah,
with all my love and affection.

CHAPTER 1

As I woke up in my double bed in my beautiful bedroom situated at the back of the house, I looked out towards the window. The curtains were pulled back as usual, and I could see that dawn was breaking. It was a beautiful, calm day in March. My husband, Gerald Derby, was still asleep in his double bed in his bedroom, which was along the landing at the front of the house.

Today was my fortieth birthday and my twentieth wedding anniversary. You could call this day anything you wanted—birthday, wedding anniversary, or something else—but the fact is it was just another day. Every day, from dawn until dusk, was always the same—a nothingness of empty days and empty nights.

I had no past to look back onto. There was nothing in my past to look back on. In the present, every day was the same—nothing to get excited about. The future had nothing to offer me. It was just the same old, same old.

There was nothing to plan for—nothing to look forward to. My life was one great boring disappointment.

As I lay there in my bed, *I thought, I have to change my life. I have to get a life. From today, my fortieth birthday, I have to promise myself that enough is enough and I am strong and capable of changing everything around me. I will definitely leave my husband, and I will fight for my house.*

I was born Pauline Ann Jackson. I was born in the house that I still lived in. As I was an only child, my parents, Joan and Tom Jackson, spoiled me. They brought me up appreciating all good values. They loved me, and I loved them.

As a young child, I was extremely quiet. I lived in my own make- believe world. I did not make friends easily. When I did have a friend at school, my parents never wanted me to bring her back to the house to play. I was never allowed to attend sleepovers. Soon I found that girls and boys at my primary school did not want to play with me, so I became a loner. I did have one friend—a makebelieve friend called Jailey. Jailey has stayed with me all my years. Even now, when I am stressed or I need help of any kind, I will talk to my beautiful friend Jailey. Could it be that she was my guardian angel?

I had a cousin called Emma. Emma was my father's brother's daughter, and she was the same age as me. We grew up together. As family, Emma was always staying with me, and I was always staying at her house. Emma was, like me, an only child. We were extremely close. We became like sisters. We even had the same surname:

Jackson. I had no friends, but I did have Cousin Emma.

In those early days, I looked terrible. I was taller than most for my age and was very thin and lanky. I had long blonde hair usually made into two plaits. I considered myself ugly. I had no self-confidence, so I remained a very quiet girl throughout my younger days.

Nothing changed in my secondary school days. If I managed to make friends, I was not allowed to bring friends home and was never allowed any sleepovers. I was not even allowed to go to other friends' homes, and as a result, I soon found myself with no friends at all. But I always had Cousin Emma.

I went through my teenage years quite happy with my own company and, of course, Jailey's company. Without Jailey, I would have been terribly lonely. Emma was always there if I needed her.

By the time I was sixteen, I had grown into quite a good-looking young lady. I was tall and slim with long blonde hair, and I had beautiful green eyes. Boys at school were getting interested in me, and I had a few dates to enjoy going on. They were always friendly dates. Never, ever, would I allow any sexual nonsense.

After secondary school, I insisted that I would not be happy going to college, so my parents agreed that I should find an apprenticeship. To my astonishment, the local photographer Roger Seymour did indeed offer me an apprenticeship.

I enjoyed working with Roger. We worked together on the local paper, weddings, christenings, and the like.

It was in my first year working and training with Roger that I met Gerald Derby. He was to become my husband.

When I was seventeen, my beautiful mother died suddenly. My father and I were devastated. From then on, my life changed. My father gave up on life. I carried on working with Roger, and the rest of the time I took care of my father. My father died when I was eighteen.

As an only child, I inherited everything. I then owned the beautiful large house that I was born in, a considerable amount of land that surrounded the house, and a considerable amount of money.

Within two years of my father's death, Gerald and I were married and he moved into my house.

So there I was, on my fortieth birthday and my twentieth wedding anniversary, living in the same house that I was born in.

"Come on, sleepyhead! Time for you to get dressed and come and have your breakfast. It is going to be a busy day for you and me today!" shouted Gerald from the kitchen.

I slowly got out of bed, showered, and dressed. Gerald had purchased me a new dress and jacket for today's celebrations—a beautiful green dress and matching fancy jacket. Even though I had not chosen it, it was truly beautiful. I had some wonderful jewellery that complemented it. I always wore stockings and a suspender belt, and I never wore a bra—only silk slips. I had a firm body; long, slender legs; firm breasts; long blonde hair; good facial features; and beautiful green eyes. Some people would say that I was quite a stunner. I loved wearing high-heeled shoes.

When I was dressed and had put my make-up on, I made my way downstairs to the kitchen.

"At last. Your breakfast is going to be ruined," remarked Gerald. "Have your breakfast first, and then we can open all the cards and presents that have arrived."

Gerald fussed over me all the time. The problem I had with Gerald was that even though he was at times a very considerate husband, over the years he had become a very controlling husband. My husband had become a manipulative, cruel husband, and I hated him.

As I ate my breakfast, I watched him clearing the dirty dishes away into the dishwasher.

Gerald was still a fine figure of a man. He stood six feet two inches tall and had curly ginger-brown hair, dark brown eyes, and a good manly body on him. He was a very handsome man. Even though he still looked good, I was not attracted to him at all.

I recalled the day we met. I was nearly seventeen years old, I was training with Roger Seymour. At a wedding we were working at, on Roger's instructions, I had to go around and ask all the immediate wedding party members to take their positions on the church steps. I politely asked the best man, who turned out to be Gerald Derby, to return to the church steps for the wedding photographs. Gerald replied, "If I do as you ask, will you let me have a date with you?" That was the beginning of our very long relationship. We were married after I had lost both my mother and my father. We were both twenty years old. We moved into my house, and twenty years on we were still living in my house.

Even though I was not at all hungry, I had to make the effort to eat the breakfast that Gerald had cooked. If I had not eaten it all, Gerald would have turned nasty and demanded that I finish every single mouthful. Today of all days, I did not want any unpleasantness, so I ate it all.

"I am pleased you enjoyed your breakfast," remarked Gerald. "We have such a busy day ahead of us. I was concerned that you would not be able to eat properly before tonight."

Typical Gerald—always looking out for me, whether I wanted him to or not.

As Gerald cleared the table and brought out all the cards and presents, he turned to me and said, "Have you forgotten something?"

"No, I don't think so. Your anniversary present is with the others," I said quietly.

"You have not wished me a happy anniversary, and more to the point, you have not kissed me!"

I began to feel sweaty and sick. Surely he was not going to start a fight today, of all days.

"Sorry, love. I am so excited I did not think," I hastily answered.

"Of course you are excited, and rightly so. Come here and let me hold you."

Oh no! I thought. Any physical or intimate contact with Gerald made my skin crawl. I hated any physical or intimate contact with my husband.

Gerald held me close as he kissed me seductively on my lips. I returned his kiss and pretended to enjoy the moment. If I had not responded to his advances, he would have continued with them until I did respond. I found that life was easier when I pretended to enjoy his kissing me and the like. The truth was the complete opposite. I hated all aspects of physical and intimate relations with Gerald, but I did not dare show that.

"You feel so lovely and sexy. I can't wait for tonight, when we will be on our own. Now let us open our cards and presents," instructed Gerald.

We had received some lovely cards and presents for our twentieth wedding anniversary, and I had received many cards and presents for my fortieth birthday. Gerald had bought me a diamond eternity ring as a joint birthday and anniversary present. It was gorgeous. I, in return, had bought him a gold watch.

Obviously, I had made quite a fuss over the ring, and I expressed my delight at it. On the other hand, Gerald was not so pleased with his gold watch.

"I told you that I was saving up for a Rolex watch and that one day I would have enough money saved up to buy one!" shouted Gerald.

"I know that, Gerald, but until you have enough saved, I thought you would like this watch, as you really need a new watch," I replied.

"Take it back and get your money back. I do not want it; I don't even like it. Put the money towards my Rolex," demanded Gerald.

That was it! The day was spoilt! For the rest of the day, Gerald sulked and was horrible to me. Nothing new there, then. Every day was a battleground. I was so sick and fed up of living a lie. To the outside world, we were the perfect couple. The reality behind our closed door was that Gerald loved his life and was always controlling me; as for me, I hated my life, and I had done so for many years.

Over the years, Gerald had built up a business selling building materials and hiring machines out for the construction industry. Not long after we were married, Gerald insisted that I give up working with Roger the photographer and start working with him in the offices of his building yard. I fought very hard to keep my position with Roger, but Gerald was such a force to reckon with that eventually I left Roger and started working with Gerald. "Anything for a calm, quiet life" became my motto then. As a result, not only did I live with Gerald, but I also worked with him. As the years went by, I lost my escape route.

On several occasions, I prepared a strategy for leaving and starting a new life. On four occasions, I told Gerald that I wanted to leave and start a life of my own. I asked him to listen to me and for us to part amiably. I explained to him that I no longer loved him and that I wanted a divorce. I had prepared everything I needed, including making sure that I had enough money in my bank account to give me a good start. I once left before contacting him to ask for him to sort things out, including my house.

On each occasion, it was a bad mistake. Gerald would have none of it. He blocked my leaving in so many ways. For example, he removed money from my bank account and placed it in our joint account and then took me off the bank signatory mandate. He refused to give me a divorce, and he always promised that we would be fine again after he had amended his ways. No, that was never the case! He became more controlling. He took my car away and sold it. I demanded that I have my own car, but he insisted that one car between us would be enough. He took me to and collected me from everywhere I wanted to go. He refused to let me go anywhere on my own. He was nasty to my dear cousin Emma to the point where she stopped visiting us. We always shopped online, for everything from food to clothes.

He was always with me at home and then at work, apart from when he went out socialising on his own. Gerald loved his pub life. Most days, after we had finished at work he would take me home so I could prepare an evening meal and clean up; and then several hours later, he would return by taxi, usually drunk. He would collect the car the following morning.

Gerald always treated me with love and affection even when he was drunk, so although I did not love him, I continued to live with him in my beautiful house—the house I was born in. Whatever decisions I was to make with regard to leaving Gerald, I had to make sure that I did not lose my house.

The day of our anniversary, Gerald and I travelled to work in the same car, as we did every other weekday. He was still sulking over the watch I had bought him for our wedding anniversary.

"Stop this nonsense now, Gerald! I shall send the watch back, and I will get you something else. Okay?" I said, talking through my teeth.

"No! You are right. I do need a watch—especially for work. My old watch has seen better days. Anyway, we do not want to spoil our day, do we?" said Gerald.

The day at work went so fast, and as a reception was being held for us at our local pub, I refreshed my make-up. Gerald was, like me, all dressed and ready for the celebrations.

After work, we made our way directly to our local pub. We arrived not long after six o clock, and I was amazed by the number of guests who had already arrived.

Friends, relatives, and colleagues had all been invited. The relatives were all Gerald's relatives. The only relatives I had were my cousin Emma and her husband, Jeff. Thank goodness, they had come along to wish us all the best. I did not know many of the people there. The only friends I knew were the couples who socialised with Gerald and me.

The buffet was brilliant. There was a band booked, and once the music started, the atmosphere was electric.

Gerald made his way to the bar, where he would stay all night. I circulated and eventually rested at my cousin Emma's table.

"How are things with you?" asked Emma. "I have not seen you for quite some while."

"Same as same as!" I replied. "I would like to meet you soon, as I want to discuss something with you."

"Any time, Pauline. You know I am always here for you.

I hope you are coming to your senses and that you are going to leave Gerald. Is that what you are thinking of doing?" asked Emma.

"I have to make many decisions, and I need someone to help me sort things out. I am so concerned that unless I do things properly, I might lose my house; but tonight is not the time to dwell on those things. I will phone you, and we shall meet up," I said quietly.

My house was a beautiful five-bedroom Georgian style house. When I married Gerald, he moved in and we made some alterations. We added bathroom en suites to all the bedrooms, a new kitchen diner, and full central heating; extended the lounge; and installed double patio doors to gain access to a large new patio. Other alterations were made, too many to mention, and I paid for the work, including fitments and fittings, out of a sum of money my parents had left me. I had no intention of losing my house.

As I sat with Emma and Jeff, the music from the band had everyone dancing, and as I looked around the room, I noticed a very handsome man standing by the stage. He was of medium height and had greying hair, but it was his smile I noticed the most. He was busy talking and laughing with other people.

"Who is that man stood near the stage talking to the landlord?" I asked Emma.

"No idea. I have not seen him before; perhaps it is one of Gerald's cousins," replied Emma.

I turned to see if everyone was making the most of the buffet, and as I turned back to talk to Emma, the gentleman in question was standing there in front of me.

"Care for a dance?" he asked. As he had such a beautiful smile on his face, I could not resist.

"Yes, I think I will." I replied, and I followed him onto the dance floor. I say it was a dance floor but it was simply the floor of a large pub. They had removed all the tables from the centre of one of the larger rooms and made a stage for the band, of course leaving enough room for dancing.

We had just reached the dancing area when the music tempo changed.

Jive music started, and my new partner said, "Want to have a go?" "Of course; why not," I replied. I was so excited.

We jived brilliantly together. We both laughed and danced and then laughed and danced some more. When the tempo changed, we made our way off the dance area.

"Hi, I am Ross. I thought we were pretty good dancing then," he said.

"I am Pauline, and yes, we did okay," I replied. "Would you like a drink?" Ross asked.

"Thank you, but not at this moment. I need to return to my cousin. Thank you for the dancing, though; I really enjoyed it." I then returned to Emma and Jeff.

Emma was laughing at me. "You looked like you were enjoying yourself there."

"Do you know, Emma, I was!" I laughed with her.

The music stopped, and Gerald and I were called onto the stage. The landlord wished me a happy birthday and both of us a happy anniversary. Gerald made a short speech, thanking everyone for coming, and then we both made our way off the stage.

"I have had enough now. Go and get your coat. There is a taxi waiting for us outside," said Gerald.

"It is not that lat. Why do you want to go now? If you were with all your drinking pals, it would be a lot later than this before you set back home!" I retorted.

"Need you ask? You showed yourself up dancing. You have had too much to drink. I do not want you to show me up any more than you have done," replied Gerald.

I had only had three drinks. I knew he was angry that I had been dancing—and of course that I had been dancing with a man. I was not in the mood to start arguing. I just wanted to get back home. Gerald had just spoilt the whole night. In fact, he had spoilt the whole day and night. Nothing new there, then.

We sat in silence in the taxi, and when we arrived home, I just went upstairs to the sanctuary of my bedroom.

I loved my bedroom. I had a television to watch my programs. I could listen to my music on my computer, and the best thing of all was that I did not need to sleep with Gerald.

We were married when we were both twenty. In those days, sex before marriage was frowned upon, and like most other couples, Gerald and I had not had sex before our wedding night.

I found Gerald very attractive, and of course I loved him, but I was surprised to find out on our wedding night that sex was not what I thought it was going to be like.

I tried to respond to Gerald's lovemaking, but there was nothing there to get me excited. As the saying goes, "He did not light my fire." Gerald was very patient and told me it takes time for a couple to blend together when it comes to sex. I truly believed that with practise over time, we would have a happy marital sex life. No such luck! I believed that I was frigid, and eventually Gerald began enjoying himself having sex with me with no foreplay or any consideration for me at all. Sex, to me, was just something one had to put up with after marriage.

As the years went by and Gerald's snoring became louder and louder, we agreed that separate bedrooms would be better all round. I was thrilled that I no longer needed to sleep with him, but it did not stop the sex, which took place twice a week on average. On those occasions, I would hear Gerald walking across the landing from his bedroom to mine. He would walk straight in, take his clothes off, and demand that I remove my clothes, and then he would have sex with me. He was usually drunk, and he smelled terrible. After, he would return to his bedroom, fall asleep, and snore all night. I would shower to clean myself, and the shower also hid my tears.

As the years went by, I could not stand him touching me. I hated the intercourse. I felt physically sick. No amount of excuses on my behalf would stop the inevitable.

When we had been married for a couple of years, I was concerned that I had not fallen pregnant. I longed for a baby. Our GP sent me to the hospital for fertility tests, and all was well with me. When it came time for Gerald to go and have the tests, he refused.He said he was content for it to be just him and me if a child did not come along. I tried and tried to persuade him to go and take the tests but he would not, and the arguments that this caused made me eventually give up pleading with him to go and be tested. I hated him for being so stubborn and selfish.

That night, after we returned from celebrating our wedding anniversary and my birthday, I was relieved to be back in my bedroom. I was warm and cosy, but inside I felt nothing but despair. I was fretful, and I knew I was going to cry. I dried my eyes, blew my nose, took a deep breath, and put my pyjamas on. I had just curled up in bed when I heard Gerald walking across the landing.

I froze, knowing what was going to happen next. Gerald came into my room and told me to take my clothes off, and after removing his clothes, he climbed into my bed.

"I told you to take your clothes off!" shouted Gerald.

"Gerald, I am not in the mood tonight. I do not want to row with you, but I feel upset; and to be honest, I feel rather sick."

"Serves you right for drinking too much," he said smugly. "Now take your clothes off and get back into bed. It is our anniversary, you know. I have been looking forward to this all night."

"No. Not toni—"

Before I could finish my sentence, Gerald had grabbed my arms and pulled me down onto the bed. He was so rough with me. At first I tried to fight him off, but it was futile. He managed to tear my pyjama pants, and with his lips firmly on mine and his hands pulling at my breasts, he started to have intercourse with me. He was hurting me, so I just lay there, waiting for it to be over. He was in such a rage, and I honestly believe that he was enjoying forcing himself upon me.

After he finished, he stood up, collected his clothes off the floor, and then turned to me and said, "Actually that was quite good, for a change." With that said, he left the room.

Then I cried. I showered to clean myself, and I cried and cried. I curled up in bed and thought, for a second time that day, I have to change my life. *I have to get a life. From today, my fortieth birthday, I have to promise myself that enough is enough and that I am strong and capable of changing everything around me. I will definitely leave my husband, and I will fight for my house.*

CHAPTER 2

Decision Time

THE NEXT MORNING, I woke up and looked out of my bedroom window. As usual, my curtains were pulled back so I could see the dawn. I could hear the birds singing. I woke with a very heavy heart. There was no going back on the decision I had made. From that day, everything I did was to help me leave Gerald. Nothing was going to stop me. As I finished dressing, Gerald shouted me from the kitchen. "Your breakfast is ready! Are you coming for it now?"

I did not answer. I made my way downstairs and into the kitchen. "I am not coming into work today, Gerald. Lynn is more than capable of taking over my tasks," I said.

Lynn was a young girl whom we had trained in our office for her college course. She was more than ready to take on more responsibilities.

"What the hell are you going to do today? I need the car; don't forget!" shouted Gerald.

I remained silent, and eventually Gerald left the house, slamming the door as he left.

I lost no time in searching the Internet for a female solicitor who specialised in marriage breakups and divorces. At last I found one in our local town. One quick phone call and I had an appointment booked for later that afternoon. I made another quick phone call to a local taxi firm and instructed them to come and pick me up straight away. I then called my cousin Emma to tell her I was on my way to see her. I collected some of my personal papers, my passport, my driving licence, and the like, and off I went in the taxi to Emma's.

Emma was not in the least surprised at my decision to leave my husband, Gerald. In fact, she was surprised that after several failed attempts at leaving Gerald I had waited so long before trying again.

"You will have all the help we can give you. Do you want to move in with us now?" asked Emma.

"No, thank you. I intend to take my time—to do everything by the book. This time I have no intention of failing. I am so excited at the prospect of starting a whole new way of life. To do that, I need to secure as much money as I can. I am hoping that my meeting with the solicitor this afternoon will provide me with all the answers I need—especially with regard to what monies I would be entitled to."

"What are you going to do about transport?" asked Emma.

"For the time being, I am content to use taxis. I have arranged for the taxi to return here and take me to the solicitor's this afternoon. If it is all right with you and Jeff, I would like to stay here until then. I need to compose myself and make a list of questions that need answering. A cup of tea and a biscuit would be great now, though." We both laughed at that.

Every now and again, Gerald would phone me on my mobile. I did not answer. I had nothing to say to him—not yet anyway.

As I entered the solicitor's office, I was so nervous that I felt physically sick. Within minutes of meeting the solicitor, a Mrs. Ruth Jones, I was completely put at my ease.

For the following two hours, I told Mrs. Jones everything about my husband and my twenty years of marriage. I told her that I needed answers—answers to help me leave my husband and divorce him, and eventually for me to start a new life—something I had longed for, over such a long time!

Mrs. Ruth Jones listened in silence. When I had finished rabbiting on, she told me there would be no problem divorcing Gerald, on several grounds. It was my decision whether to insist that I remain in the property; she could arrange to ask Gerald to leave, legally. It would make no sense for us both to continue to live at the same property.

With regard to me wanting to safeguard the house for myself, Mrs. Jones said there were several ways that we could do that, but that would only be discussed when the divorce was on its way through, and all assets, including those of the business, would have to be taken into account. I agreed with her and gave her the instruction to start divorce proceedings. I arranged to tell her as soon as possible whether it would be me or Gerald that remained living in our house.

As I was about to leave the solicitor's office, someone called out, "Pauline?" I turned, and there was Ross, the man I had met the previous night.

"Hello, fancy meeting you here!" I said. I could feel my face flushing and my heart beating ever so loudly.

"Well, yes, considering that I work here!" answered Ross, and we both laughed.

"I was just leaving after an appointment with a Mrs. Ruth Jones," I said. "So, you work here, then?"

"For my sins, I am also a solicitor here. Do you fancy a coffee? I am just going for a late afternoon coffee and a snack, and I would love the company."

I nodded, and we both left the offices. As we walked along the town streets, we chatted, and I think that he was flirting with me. I found him deliciously attractive. Ross was of medium height and was a little plump. He had slightly greying brown hair, blue eyes, and a most inviting smile, and he was in my age group.

Ross and I chatted about everything, but we never mentioned why I had been to see Mrs. Jones. I enjoyed coffee and cake, and all too soon it was time for Ross to return to his work.

"Are you walking back my way?" asked Ross.

"Sadly, no. I thank you for a very relaxing time. I needed that!" I exclaimed.

"Are you married, Ross?" I asked.

"Well, in a way. Are you happily married, Pauline?" asked Ross.

"Well, not exactly!" I replied.

"Right! This calls for me to take your phone number.

Do you agree?" asked Ross.

"I most certainly do!" I answered. We both laughed and giggled as I gave him my number.

I walked around the town's streets for quite a while. I was elated. I was not sure if I was elated because I had made the decision to start divorce proceedings or because I had been entertained by the lovely Ross. For the first time in a long time, I felt alive and excited at my future prospects.

I returned home just as Gerald was pulling up at the house.

"Where the hell have you been all bloody day?" was the greeting he gave me.

I did not answer. I made my way into the kitchen, took my coat off, and waited for him to come in. Before he could give me any more verbal abuse, I told him that I had started divorce proceedings and that there was no way I was going to change my mind this time.

Gerald was extremely angry. He said what he wanted to say and then left to go to the pub with his friends.

I knew it was futile to ask Gerald to leave the marital home—my house. I had to make the decision that I would leave. I packed my things—the things I would need for the foreseeable future—and called a taxi and made my way to Emma's house.

Emma and her husband, Jeff, made me so welcome. Emma gave me the use of one of their bedrooms, and after a drink or two with them both, I retired to my new home for the time being.

CHAPTER 3

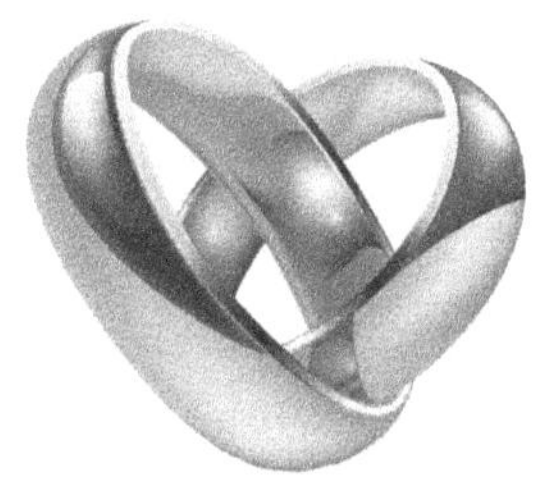

Freedom

Sleep did not come easy that night. The happy feelings I had experienced that day slowly melted away. I was alone in someone else's home. I was so unhappy inside. I was worried about my future. I was worried about Gerald. I knew I had to stay strong and go through with the divorce. I could not give in and go back to the house. I did not know how long it would take. Would I have enough money to live well? Eventually I fell into a deep sleep, and when I awoke the following morning, although I still felt uneasy about my situation, I knew I had the strength to carry on. Before I had dressed, Gerald was waiting for me in Emma's kitchen. I dreaded seeing him. I dreaded talking to him.

Gerald greeted me with "Right! Stop this nonsense now. Come home and we will discuss what has really upset you."

"I want a divorce, and I have started the proceedings," I said calmly. "You will receive the papers, and you will have up to eight days to return the acknowledgment-of-service form. If you defend the divorce, a court will hear our case and rule on it. If I do not get a divorce through now, I will wait until we have lived apart for two years, and I will apply for one then, and of course I will be granted that one. I have no intention of returning to our house. I have decided to move on. You know I do not love you and have not loved you for years. I don't think you really love me, so I am doing both of us a favour. And before you ask, my grounds for the divorce are your unreasonable behaviour."

"I know things have not been right between us for some time, but we can try to change things and work things out. What do you expect to get financially out of all this, because I have no intention of losing the business because of you!"

"I have no intention of ruining you; all I want is what is rightfully mine. We will discuss this at a later time, but please believe me when I say that I have left you for good."

Gerald was so angry. He stormed out of Emma's kitchen, and then I heard him drive away. I was shaking from head to foot, but I was very calm.

Gerald did return the acknowledgment-of-service form, and he did state that he would defend the divorce. My solicitor explained to me that there would be a court hearing and that the court would decide on the divorce. If I was successful, I would be given a decree nisi, and then six weeks later I could apply for a decree absolute.

I knew it would probably be months before my divorce case reached court, so I carried on making plans for my future.

As the weeks went by, I stayed with Emma and Jeff. When Emma and Jeff went to their cottage in France, I went with them. They stopped in France for the following six months, but I stayed there for only a month.

I had a wonderful time in France. I met some very interesting people. I rested well, I ate well, and I ended up with a lovely tan. I looked pretty good, even if I said that myself.

When I returned home to Emma's house, there was a letter waiting for me from the court. They had agreed in principal to my divorce, and subject to an agreement with Gerald to divide assets, they would grant me the decree nisi.

I had been living off my savings, which by that time were nearing nothing. I contacted my solicitor, who agreed to meet me and go over how Gerald and I were to divide our assets.

Gerald had completely ignored me, so with the help of my solicitor, we wrote to him with my proposals for the asset sharing. Eventually Gerald and I agreed that I was to keep my house and that he would have the business.

I was soon in possession of the decree absolute. At last I was free to start a new life.

I took my wedding ring off my finger. This ring that I had been wearing was not a ring of love. It was a ring of control! I was more than happy to take it off and throw it away.

I might have safeguarded my house, and it was now my house 100 per cent but I had no income. I knew it was time for me to seriously look for employment. I spent hours looking through newspapers, looking on employment sites on the Internet, and enrolling at the job centre to secure some help with finding some employment local to where I lived.

I prepared a CV, but there was nothing on it apart from the time I was working with Gerald. Obviously, Gerald was not going to give me a reference.

It was just by chance that one day, while out shopping in my local town, I saw a job vacancy sign in the local estate agency's window. I took a large breath and walked straight in, and within two hours, I had a job.

The job was for twenty hours per week, hours to be negotiable, and my duties were to be of an administrative nature. I was so thrilled, but the downside of this was that I had no one to tell my good news to. Within two weeks, I started my new employment—and I loved it!

The day arrived when I could return to my house.

I was so nervous entering the house. It seemed so large, cold, and empty. I had not seen Gerald for weeks. There was a rumour that he had met a woman and had started a relationship with her. Good for him; I wished him all the best for the future.

The day I moved back into my house, I received a phone call from Ross. He knew of my circumstances from what my solicitor Ruth had told him, and he was eager to meet up with me for a chat. I agreed to meet him, and by the time we had finished the telephone conversation, we had agreed that he would pick me up on the following Saturday; he was to take me for an Indian meal followed by a few drinks. Yes! I thought.

I had taken a few days off work so I would have plenty of time to take stock of what I needed to do to the house and unpack what few belongings I had.

I wandered around from room to room. The house was so large, and it seemed so quiet. I looked at all my old clothes. There was nothing worth keeping.

I ran down the stairs and straight into the kitchen diner. I stopped quickly, and I was shocked to see Gerald seated at my kitchen table.

"What the hell are you doing here? How did you get in?" I shouted. I was so shocked and nervous.

"There is no need for you to greet me like that! The back door was open, and I shouted, but you must not have heard me!" exclaimed Gerald.

"I have two sets of keys. Have you any more copies of the house keys?" I asked quietly.

"No. You have all the house keys!" exclaimed Gerald, but I knew that the back door was locked when I entered my house for the first time after the divorce settlement.

"What do you want, Gerald?" I asked politely.

"I have come in peace, to wish you all the best with moving back into your home. I should have brought you some flowers or something, but I came here on the spur of the moment."

"Thank you. Sorry I cannot offer you any tea or coffee, but I have yet to do a shop."

"No problem. I have to go now. I hope you will be happy here again.

Presumably happier than when I lived here with you!" remarked Gerald.

I was so relieved when he stood up and walked away from the table. I just wanted him to leave. It all happened so quickly! Gerald grabbed me and pushed me up against the closed back door. His lips were heavy on mine. His body was pushed up hard against my body. I tried pushing him away, but he was too strong for me. I could not say anything, as his mouth was pressed so hard against mine. Gerald pulled at my clothing as he tried to get hold of my breasts. He was rubbing his manhood up against me. I could feel his manhood, erect and hard. Gerald had his tongue in my mouth, and he had managed to get hold of my breasts, and he was hurting me as he squeezed them. I struggled and kicked out. It seemed ages before I managed to free myself of him. I was so frightened he was going to hurt me.

I ran into the hallway, ready to make my exit through the front door, and then I heard the back kitchen door open and bang shut. I waited, listening for any sounds from the kitchen, but there were none. I noticed that Gerald's car was not in my driveway. He must have parked on the main road or walked along the road or through the field at the back of the house.

I was very shaken up. I slowly looked into the kitchen. There was no sign of him, so I ran to the back door and locked it with my key and bolted the bolt at the top of the door.

After I had composed myself, I went out shopping. I had a huge list of things I needed to purchase, so I phoned a taxi to take me to town. I had originally thought it would be pleasant to walk through the countryside to town, but Gerald had frightened the life out of me, so I thought it safer to go by taxi.

A few hours later, I returned by taxi to the house. I had managed to purchase many of the things from my list, and I had only a few more things to get another day.

I was very tired, so apart from placing my food shop in the fridge, opening the new bedding package, and making the bed, I decided to leave all the other packages until another time.

That night, I curled up in my beautiful bed. The new bedding was so crisp and clean. I lay there listening to the silence of the house. The house seemed even more cold and huge than before.

I had so many good memories there, but that night I had more bad memories than good to think back upon.

I drifted into an uneasy sleep. I was startled by a loud noise, and as it had woken me up, I lay there listening for any other noises. I faintly heard footsteps. They seemed to be coming from downstairs—possibly in the hall. I tried to listen more intently, but my heart was pounding so loudly it stopped me from hearing anything properly.

I then heard the footsteps again. This time I could tell they were in the kitchen. I heard the fridge door open and then close. I was completely freaked out. I grabbed my phone and my dressing gown and ran into my shower room, where I locked the door and then dialled 999.

When prompted by the operator, I told him what was happening. He instructed me to stay where I was and told me that when the police arrived they would make themselves heard to me, and then I could leave where I was to let the police officers in—but only if it was safe to do so.

I was so frightened. I was frightened to think that I had an intruder. I was more frightened to think that Gerald was the culprit and that he had come to attack me again. I could not think straight. I knew that I had bolted the back door, so if it was Gerald, he must have had another set of keys and gained entry by way of the front door.

It seemed such a long time before I heard the police officers calling to me. I ran as fast as I could out of the shower room and down the stairs. I opened my front door, where I collapsed crying into the arms of a policewoman.

During the following hour, the police searched upstairs, downstairs, and all outside. They found nothing. They sat me down when I was calm enough to listen to them, and they told me that perhaps it was just my imagination playing tricks on me—especially as it was my first night back there and I was all on my own. They said everywhere was locked up so there was no forced entry. I did not dare tell them about Gerald, because if they had subsequently interviewed him, he would have been furious, and then he really would have made my life a misery.

As I was talking to the police, I noticed one of the police officers bolting my back door. I shouted to him and asked him if he had unbolted it, and when he answered no, I tried to explain to them that I had definitely bolted that door before I had gone to bed. Nobody was really listening to me, but I knew then that Gerald must have entered through the front door and made his exit through the back door after he had unbolted it.

The final piece of advice the police could give me was that to feel more secure it might be a good idea to have the locks changed. I thought to myself, *Great idea*!

When everyone had left, I nervously went upstairs to go back to bed. Then I noticed that the door to what had once been Gerald's bedroom was open wide. I knew that I had closed that bedroom door. I slowly walked across the landing—the landing that Gerald used to walk across to gain access to my bedroom and my bed. I walked into the bedroom, looked around, and then made a quick exit, making sure that I closed that door tight.

I curled up in my bed, feeling so unsure at what lay ahead of me with regard to my future. It took me a long time that night to go back to sleep.

The following morning, I was up, dressed, and ready to go. The first thing I arranged was for a locksmith to come and change all my locks. Then I cleared all the old clothes out of the wardrobes and put them in bags, ready for the charity shops. By the end of the day, I had new locks and two new sets of keys. Job done! At least I would feel safe on my own in my large house.

At last Saturday arrived. After everything that had happened to me that week, I was so looking forward to meeting up with Ross and letting him take me out to an Indian restaurant. I spent most of the day preparing my clothes, bathing, washing my hair, painting my nails, and choosing my make- up for the night.

By the time Ross turned up in his car, I was well and truly ready. In fact, I was quite excited. I found Ross to be a very handsome, pleasant man. He had a wonderful smile, and of course, we were pretty good at jiving together. Ross was about my age, greying a little, and although he was of medium height, he was also quite stocky. I wouldn't say I was attracted to him, but he was such good fun and so easy to get on with that I decided to give him a chance.

We had a wonderful night: good food, good drinks, and the company was very good. We talked and laughed all the way through the meal. We were so at ease with each other's company.

I found out that his surname was Murdock and that he was married but did not live with his wife. He said they had parted company a few years ago. He was a solicitor in the same practice as my solicitor, Ruth Jones.

When we pulled up in my driveway, I thanked Ross for a wonderful evening. Ross replied that he would love to take me out again, and I said I would love to go out with him again.

"Pauline, are you not going to ask me in for a coffee?" asked Ross. "Believe it or not Ross, I have had such a bad week, I would rather not. Not until I am straight and I can feel at ease asking you to come in for coffee."

"No problem. Perhaps we can go out for a Chinese next week, maybe Wednesday night. How does that sound?

Maybe then I could come back for coffee!" "Yes, that would be good."

Before I had chance to leave his car, Ross lunged at me to give me a goodnight kiss. I freaked out. I moved away instantly, and then I was so embarrassed by my behaviour.

"Please forgive me, Ross," I said. "I have had some very disturbing things happen to me this week. I make no excuses for my behaviour. I am afraid that I am too scared to have any physical contact. I was hoping that I would have got over this by now; unfortunately I have not."

"I think you and I need to relax and you need to talk to me. Make me understand what is happening to you. Perhaps I can help. Let us go in and have that coffee. I promise you I am a good listener.

I opened the front door, and Ross and I entered.

"It is a beautiful house, Pauline. Do you not feel lonely here? It is so large!"

"I have so many mixed emotions about this house; I honestly don't know what to say," I replied.

I made the coffee, and Ross and I made ourselves comfortable in the lounge. The fire was burning quite brightly. Ross turned the lights out, and we both sat there talking about all my fears and what had been happening to me during those recent few weeks.

"So you see, Ross, I am nowhere near ready for a new relationship," I said. "I thank you for listening to me tonight. I do not tell people about my private life, but you have made me feel quite at ease."

"Well, Pauline. You have had a pretty rough time of it over the years and a few bad experiences most recently.

Have you got anything stronger than coffee to drink?"

"Yes, I have!" I laughed at those words. "A good malt whisky. Will that do?"

"Now you are talking my language! You need to relax more and stop taking circumstances and people so seriously. Have a drink with me, relax, and I am going to make you feel so good. I know you are very nervous, but a few drinks and you know where this is going to lead. Are you up for this? Treat all this as a lesson in life, and I promise you that you will not regret this!"

I did not know what to do. I had a drink, and then I realised I did not want to lose Ross as a friend or maybe a lover. We both talked and laughed for a while. I was so nervous, but I was so inquisitive as to whether there might be something exciting on offer to me that night.

"Come on, Pauline. I want to share a bed with you for an hour or so." With that said, we went upstairs to my bedroom.

I stood there in the corner of my bedroom. I was so nervous. I waited for instructions. Ross sat on the end of my bed, and he removed his shirt. I could see his hairy chest, and I was feeling sexually aroused.

"Come here. I am not going to hurt you," whispered Ross. If you want me to stop at any time, tell me, and I promise you I will stop. Now turn the lights on full. I do not want either of us to miss out on anything." We both laughed.

I walked over to him and stood between his legs. He slowly undressed me and at intervals kissed my breasts. By the time I had lost all of my clothes, Ross was holding my breasts, squeezing them hard, and gently biting my nipples. He stood up, and his lips touched my lips. He started kissing me ever so gently, but he was soon kissing me harder. I felt his tongue on my tongue. He removed the rest of his clothes. I could see his penis, hard and erect. We both lay down on my bed. Ross made sure that he was gentle as he stroked my body. He paid particular attention to stroking my clitoris and kissing me seductively. I had no idea what I was supposed to do to Ross, but before long, Ross manoeuvred into a position on top of me. I felt his penetration. He was so gentle. He kissed me whilst moving with precision inside me. It did not take long for me to have an orgasm and for Ross to climax.

We both lay there for quite a while. I was so thrilled that I had at last achieved an orgasm. It was truly brilliant.

"Well, Pauline. Did that lesson in life impress you?" asked Ross. "You were fantastic! I never imagined it to feel so good!" I said whilst still trying to get my breath back.

"You stay there. I really do have to go. Are we still on for Wednesday night?" asked Ross.

"Oh yes, and be assured that I am looking forward to seeing you again. Good night, Ross."

Ross then left. I ran down the stairs and locked the front door. I quickly ran around the house, checking that all the doors and windows were locked. I then returned upstairs, curled up in my bed, and fell immediately into a beautiful sleep.

The next morning, I woke early. I looked out of my bedroom window as dawn was breaking, just as I had done a thousand times before; only that morning, everything was different! I was different!

By Wednesday, the whole house was looking so much better. I was looking forward to seeing Ross again. I was proud of the transformation of the house from a cold, darkish place to a light, refreshing, beautiful house.

Six o' clock came, and I was all dressed up in new clothes I had bought that day. I was excited waiting for Ross to turn up. He never came. I sat waiting, watching out of the front window, hoping to see Ross's car turn in. Stupid as it may seem, I had never asked for Ross's phone number. I had never had any need of it; but that night I wished I could get in touch with him to ask him why he had not turned up. I retired to bed with a very heavy heart. Perhaps Ross wanted more from me, or perhaps after having sex with me he was no longer interested in me. Perhaps I was no good at sexual intercourse and I was not experienced enough at sex for Ross.

The next day, I was tempted to phone him at his place of work, but sense prevailed. Just as I was thinking about him, my solicitor, Ruth Jones, phoned me.

"Hi, Mrs. Derby, I hope I find you well," said Ruth. "You asked me to call you after all the divorce and settlement were completed. You made enquiries about changing your surname back to your maiden name, Jackson. Do you still wish to proceed with this? It is a very easy process, and I can do it all for you."

"Oh yes! I am so thankful for everything you have done for me so far, and this would be the last thing I would like to complete," I replied.

"I will post out all the relevant forms for you to sign. Return them when you can," said Ruth.

"I will, but before you go, I was wondering if you had a solicitor there called Ross Murdock?" I asked.

"Yes, Ross works here. Do you know him?"

"Only in passing. Sorry, I was just being inquisitive; perhaps I should not have asked about him," I said quite apologetically.

Ruth was quiet at the other end of the phone. "What I can tell you, Mrs. Derby, is that Ross does have a bit of a reputation for liking women. Pity, because he has a lovely wonderful wife who is expecting their first child. Please do not repeat anything I have just told you. Good day, Mrs. Derby. I will pop the papers in the post for you." Ruth then hung up.

I was upset, because I had thought I was beginning to get a life for myself, but all that I had achieved was to find myself duped by the first man who showed an interest in me, only to find that this man was interested in only one thing—sex. I was so stupid!

I did see Ross again, though only in passing; and he was polite to me, and I to him. The bastard!

I decided that from then on I did not need or want a man in my life. I could live quite easily without a man. I had no interest in men at all!

Christmas was only a couple of weeks away, and I had made the effort to buy and decorate a Christmas tree. I was still enjoying my part-time employment at the estate agency in town. I was becoming a very lonely person.

I purchased a small car, but I was never in the mood to go out and meet new friends. My cousin Emma was the only person I had any time for. I loved Emma, and she understood me. She was most insistent that I spend Christmas Day with them, and I gratefully accepted the invitation.

Christmas Eve was a nightmare for me. I was so lonely and depressed. I wandered alone around the house. I had a beautiful Christmas tree, but no one was going to see it. I had thought of inviting Emma and her husband, Jeff, for Boxing Day, but Emma had told me that they had been invited elsewhere.

At last Christmas Day came. I put on my Christmas jumper and matched up a skirt and shoes. I locked the house up and drove to Emma's house.

"Merry Christmas, Pauline!" shouted Emma from her kitchen. "Merry Christmas, Emma and Jeff!" I shouted back.

"I hope you are hungry!" Emma shouted.

I laughed and eagerly accepted a glass of wine from Jeff.

"I have your presents here, Emma. Do you want them now?" I asked. "No thank you. We will open all the presents after the Christmas dinner and after we have had a few more drinks!" said Emma, and we all laughed.

Christmas dinner was superb. Emma was such a good cook, and it was wonderful watching Emma and Jeff together. After all the years they had been married, I could still see the love they had for each other. Like me, Emma had not had any children. I envied Emma. How I would have loved to have a loving relationship with someone.

After we cleared the table, we all took our positions in the lounge for the annual giving of Christmas presents. In turn, we were presented with the relevant wrapped gifts. We all pulled and tore at the wrapping paper.

The first present I unwrapped was, to my amazement, a dog's collar and lead. I asked Emma if that was a joke present, but she would not answer me. The next present I unwrapped was two dog bowls. I laughed, and Jeff asked me to unwrap the last present, which turned out to be a dog's bed.

"Am I to presume that you are going to get me a dog?" I asked.

"No," said Jeff. "We already have him here. Do you want to meet him?"

I was so excited and a little apprehensive. "Go on then!" I replied. Emma opened the kitchen door, and in came bounding a large black bundle of puppy. For a few moments, he caused mayhem.

Eventually I caught hold of him, and as he looked at me with the most beautiful black eyes, I fell in love with him immediately.

"He is a Labrador pup, ten weeks old. You have to train him from the start," said Jeff.

I was speechless. I just sat on the floor holding this wonderful bundle of joy. The pup was tired and fell asleep in my arms.

"Emma thought that a dog in your life will not only protect you but will give you a reason to get up the morning, so to speak," said Jeff.

I was so excited and so thankful to Emma and Jeff, and I refused any more wine, as I just wanted to take my pup home immediately.

When I arrived home, I placed the dog's bed in the kitchen. Brutus was going to be his name—a name that was strong and noble. I must have spent an hour walking him up and down the back garden, waiting for him to wee and poo. Eventually I brought him back into the kitchen, fed and watered him, and settled him down into his bed. But before I could make my escape from the kitchen, Brutus had run up the stairs and jumped up on to my bed. I chased him up the stairs, and by the time I entered my bedroom, Brutus was fast asleep.

That night I curled up with my beautiful Brutus. From that night, Brutus always insisted that he curl up in my bed to sleep.

I woke the following morning early. As usual, I looked out of my bedroom window to watch the dawn, only that morning was somewhat special. I was not alone!

CHAPTER 4

Moving On

Summer was upon us. Brutus was a large black Labrador dog—not yet fully grown, but he was a beauty. He meant everything to me. He had completely changed my life for the better.
I enjoyed taking him out every day. I met new people—usually people who were themselves taking their dogs out for exercise.

Apart from work, I took Brutus with me everywhere. He ate with me. He slept with me. At night he would curl up on the rug in the lounge while I read or watched television. He was the love of my life.

Gerald had called upon me several times, and he even played with Brutus. Gerald seemed pleasant, and he told me that he was in a relationship with an older woman but said he was happy, so I wished him well.

I had come to terms with the fact that my house was far too big for Brutus and me, but I had no idea what to do about it. I had fought hard to retain the ownership of my family home, and now I knew it was just a house. In fact, I had more bad memories than good memories in the house.

I had no idea what to do about my house until one day, as I was looking on the computer at work, I came across a small cottage for sale. I read the description and details of this pretty little cottage. The photograph showed it as a pretty chocolate-box cottage—very old. It had a middle front door with a small window on either side and three small windows on firsr floor. A few feet of garden led to the charming front gate, and the description stated that it had a huge garden to the rear. It held two bedrooms, a lounge, a kitchen diner, and an inglenook fireplace, and it had central heating. It was a joy just looking at the photograph and reading the description.

There was a big downside to all my enthusiasm. The cottage was hundreds of miles away, on the east coast of southern Scotland.

For days, I could not stop thinking about that cottage. When I was at work and nobody was watching me, I would bring the cottage up on the computer screen.

The price I could sell my house for exceeded the cost of the cottage. I knew that if I went ahead with the transaction, I would have quite a tidy sum of money left over. There would be no need for me to work for a while.

I mentioned it to the girls at work, but they said that it was miles away from anywhere, so for a while I gave up on the idea of moving. But I made a note of the address of the cottage and noted its postal code. I thought, *Well, you never know*!

Sure enough, one bright Sunday morning, I could not help myself. I packed a picnic, made a flask of hot tea, and prepared Brutus some food and some water, and both Brutus and I set off on our adventure!

I had programmed the satellite navigation, so all I had to do was enjoy the ride. It was several hours before we reached the nearest town to the cottage. I stopped at a garage to purchase a local map, just in case the satellite navigation could not find me the cottage.

As I thought, the sat navigated us to a long, winding country road, but there was no cottage to be seen anywhere. In fact, there were no residences anywhere. I stopped for a while to read the local map. I had already driven down that country road for several miles, and according to the map I still had quite a way to go.

I continued driving. "Well, Brutus, at this rate we will be at the coast soon," I said. "That would be brilliant if there was a beach nearby to take our walks on!"

Then I noticed the cottage on the left. I pulled up alongside the cottage. My, how beautiful it was! Across the road, just before the road veered left, there were large gates and a tall walled area that seemed to go on for miles. The only sign I could see was a plaque on the gate, which read, "Formby Estate" and "Private".

I was so nervous and excited. I got out of the car and slowly walked over to the cottage. It was even more beautiful than I had imagined it would be.

I opened the small gate and walked up to the front door.

The name "The Cottage" was inscribed into the wood. I knocked on the door, but no one answered. I had my doubts that anyone lived there, but I did not want to be rude and start looking through the windows.

As I started to walk back to my car, a large black Lexus drove up to the tall gates on the right-hand side of the road. The driver looked my way, and for a moment, our eyes met. Sexual electricity went all through my body. I had never experienced anything so powerful before. I was thinking about interrupting the driver to ask him if he knew if anyone lived at the cottage, but the powerful feelings I had encountered stopped me. The Lexus drove through the open gates, and the gates closed behind it.

I got in my car and continued along the country road. The whole area around was nothing but fir trees and fields. The large wall on the right-hand side of the road continued for several miles, until it became a large wooden fence. Eventually the road just ended, and the large wooden fence veered left and continued through wooded areas.

I stopped the car where the road ended. Brutus and I walked around outside the car. I could see through the wooden fence that there was indeed a beach area. We were actually on the coast. There was no access to the beach area, but Brutus and I sat by the car and had ourselves a picnic.

I was still reeling from the impact of the one brief moment when my eyes had looked into the eyes of a stranger. It was truly a powerful sexual experience.

After our picnic and a good walk around the area, we made our way back home—but not before I took loads and loads of photographs.

It was quite a long roundabout trip. When we arrived home, I was shattered but was also excited. I knew that it was fate that had led me to that charming little cottage. I was going to do everything in my power to buy it and move there.

The very next day, as soon as I had arrived at work, I told the office manager of my intention to sell my house and purchase the cottage. I instructed them to act on my behalf, and in due course they arranged for me to meet their counterpart at the cottage for a full viewing. That was arranged for the following weekend, and by close of business of that day, my house had been valued and was up for sale.

On the day the For Sale sign was placed outside my house, I was a little emotional. I had never expected that I would ever leave my home. It was not long before Gerald came to see me.

As he walked through the back door he said, "Well, this had better be good! I want to know what the hell you are playing at!"

"If you refer to the selling of my house, I am moving away. I need to start a new life away from this place," I replied.

"Pauline, we have had some wonderful times here. Are you absolutely sure that you and I could not start over again? I love you, and I know that you love me. Give me one more chance! Let me take you out for a meal tonight, and let us talk about everything that matters. What do you say?"

"Gerald, if you love someone, they have to love you back. Love works both ways, and I am afraid that I do not love you!" I replied.

"Just come here and let me hold you. Just to prove my point," said Gerald as he moved towards me.

That was it! I was so frightened of what he might try to do that I screamed at him to leave. I must have shocked Gerald by screaming at him that way, because he turned and left straight away. I closed my door and bolted it.

Finally the day arrived for me to view the cottage. It was quite a long journey, but Brutus and I set off early, armed with a large picnic and a flask of tea.

I parked in front of the garage, which was set back a little from the cottage itself. I did not have long to wait before a gentleman from the estate agency came and unlocked the front door.

I left Brutus in the car and walked into the cottage. What I saw far exceeded what I had been expecting. It was beautiful! I was overcome by the beauty of such a small place. Every room, although old, had a magical feel to it.

The gentleman that opened the door for me said he would leave me there to look at the whole of the cottage at my leisure on the condition that I return the keys to their office before office closing time. I eagerly accepted his invitation.

Brutus and I sat in the lounge of the cottage, having the full picnic that I had brought. I laughed at my behaviour. For two hours, I went from room to room. I walked around the garden perimeter. I took what seemed like thousands of photographs. There was nothing I disliked about the whole place. I thought to myself, *Fantastic. I am going to really enjoy living here. I am going to make a new life for myself, and I am going to meet new friends and acquaintances. At last life is going to be worth living!*

Three months—that was the amount of time it took from the beginning to the end of the process of selling, buying, and receiving the keys to my very own small cottage. The downside was that I had to give up my parttime job, but I was quite well off when I sold my house and downsized. There was plenty of time before I needed to find any employment. I just wanted to enjoy the move and get myself acquainted with the surrounding area.

The cottage was so small that I had no use of most of my furniture. I hired a removals firm to collect what I was taking, and the day arrived when I met the small removals van outside my new home.

I parked in front of the small garage and left Brutus in the car. I was standing on the footpath, watching all my belongings being carried inside, when I heard someone calling to me.

"Are you moving into the cottage?" shouted someone.

I turned and glanced around. There, across the road, near the Formby estate's access road, was the black Lexus. A man was standing outside it. He was the older man that had had such a striking effect on me. He was wearing a long waxed coat and matching cap—very sporty!

I looked straight into his eyes. I could not make out what colour they were or indeed what this older man looked like because of the cap he was wearing, but again, I was not in control of the strong sexual attraction I was feeling. I stood there and stammered my reply. "Yes, I am moving in today, and I am quite excited about it!"

"Do you require any help at all?" asked the older man.

"No thank you! I think I am in full control of the situation." I stammered those words as well. With that, he touched the rim of his cap and bade me good day. He then drove away.

I was totally taken aback by the way he spoke and by the way he touched the rim of his cap whilst bidding me good day. What a gentleman! Why was I so sexually attracted to him? I had never even met this gentleman properly.

By the time evening came, the removal people had left and Brutus and I were alone in the lounge of my beautiful little cottage.

It was a little chilly, as autumn was well underway. I actually managed to light and keep alight the open fire. I must admit that I put too many logs onto the lit fire, as it was still blazing away when it was time for Brutus and me to retire to bed. My new bedding looked great, and as I curled up under the duvet, I could not stop my thoughts from drifting to "my gentleman". Even when I thought about him, I felt sexual feelings towards him.

I had never, ever encountered feelings like those before. What was I to do about them? I had no idea!

I woke the following day to the first morning in my cottage. I lay there in bed with Brutus by my side. I listened to the silence, which was broken now and again by birds singing. There was no traffic noise because there was no passing traffic.

Suddenly the sound of banging came from downstairs. I jumped out of bed, put my dressing gown, on and went down. There was someone banging on my front door, so I slowly opened it.

"Sorry to call so early, Miss Jackson, but I thought I would call on you before I opened the post office," said a very attractive woman, who seemed to look about my age.

I invited her in and apologised for not being up and for still being in my night attire when I greeted her.

"No problem. Perhaps I am a little early, for which I will apologise to you."

We both laughed.

"I am here to welcome you to our town and surrounding area. My name is Joyce Macey, and I am the local postmistress for this area. I have a small post office cum small shop on the edge of town. That is why I knew your name before we were introduced." We both laughed again. "I am also here to offer you my services as official guide for the town and surrounding area. I have brought you some literature for you to read at your leisure. I know you have relocated here from the north-west of England, and I presume that everything is completely new to you."

"You presume right, Joyce," I replied, and we both laughed again.

Joyce Macey sat with me for about half an hour. We seemed to have a good connection with one another. She was a beautiful woman, probably about my age. She remarked that I had no immediate neighbours, so she wanted to know if she could take me out for a day and maybe go for a meal and a drink so she could introduce me to some local people.

I accepted her offer without any hesitation.

"Before you go, Joyce, do you know who lives at the Formby estate?" I asked politely.

"A Professor Malcolm James McKenzie," Said Joyce. "He is a nuclear scientist. He employs a few local people: groundsmen and the like, and a housekeeper. He's a real gentleman. I believe he travels a lot. If I get the chance at the meeting at the town hall next week, I will introduce him to you. Now I really must dash! It was good to meet you. You will find my phone number somewhere in all that paperwork."

"Is there a Mrs. McKenzie?" I asked, and then I could feel myself blushing.

"Not that I am aware of, but he is a lover of women, if you understand my drift."

As Joyce made her way out of my cottage, I thanked her for her consideration, and I promised that I would be in touch once I had settled in.

CHAPTER 5

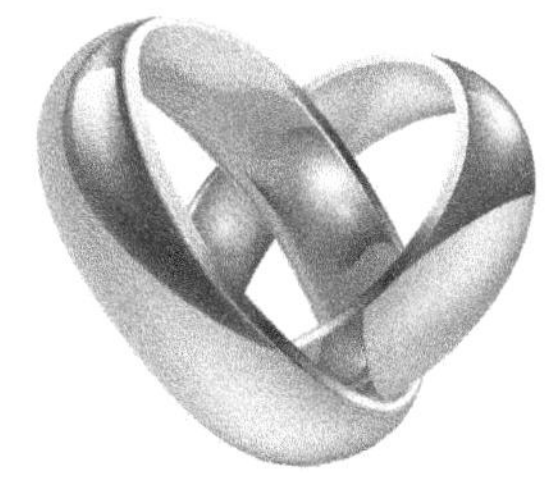

A New Home

EVERY MORNING I WOKE up in my beautiful bed, with Brutus by my side, in my little cottage. I was contented, and I was happy. I had not had time to feel lonely. I was busy unpacking and doing a little painting. The highlight of my days was taking Brutus for his daily walk. Together we walked for miles. It was not long before I knew all the surrounding area. What a joy it was!

One night I sat in front of my fire and started to read all the literature Joyce had left for me. One leaflet caught my attention immediately. It was the notice that there was going to be a meeting in the town hall to discuss the pros and cons of the construction of a large nuclear power station. The location of this power station was approximately ten miles north of the town. That was ten miles north of where I had relocated to. In honesty, I did not care about it at all, but the leaflet mentioned that Professor Malcolm James McKenzie was going to be there representing the nuclear power station.

I wanted to go to this meeting, as I thought it would give me a chance to meet the professor. One quick phone call to Joyce and it was all arranged. Joyce agreed to pick me up on the night of the meeting, and she stated she was looking forward to introducing me to good persons of interest. We both laughed.

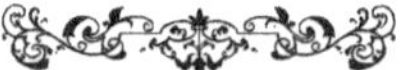

The evening of the meeting arrived. Joyce picked me up, and we drove to the town hall. I had spent most of the day getting ready, making sure that I looked my very best.

We parked up, and once we were in the room where the meeting was to be held, Joyce left me to busy herself with all the arrangements.

I sat myself down not too near the front of the stage. On the stage platform, there was a long table split into four segments, each with its own microphone. Obviously one of the segments was for the professor.

I turned to look around the large room, and then I saw Professor Malcolm James McKenzie. He was standing near the stage, talking to a very attractive woman. He had his arm around her shoulders. My heart was beating so loudly. What was it with me and this man—a man I had never met? I watched him ever so closely. I was surprised at how tall he was. He must have been well over six feet tall. He was of medium build—a balding man with grey hair. I could see his beautiful hands. He had long fingers.

I trembled at the thought of those hands touching me. This professor was smartly dressed in a suit, shirt, and tie. I could not see the colour of his eyes. All I knew was that they were responsible for the sexual attraction I had previously felt. He looked quite older than I was—maybe ten years older—but I thought he looked magnificent.

The room was beginning to fill up. On the stage, there were four representatives: one for the nuclear power station, one for the chamber of commerce, one from the school of governors, and one from the medical profession. Sheets of paper were circulating around the room. They were the official questionnaire paper for the panel. I took hold of one of said papers and completed it, providing my name and a question. I handed my paper in to the chairman and returned to my seat. I was being very brave in a strange town amongst strangers, but I just had to meet Malcolm James McKenzie. I was besotted with him though I had never met him. How bad was that? I was asking for trouble!

Not all the questionnaires were utilised, and I did not expect mine to be selected, but selected it was!

"Miss Pauline Jackson," shouted the chairman.

I stood up and said, "Good evening, Mr. Chairman and the panel. My name is Pauline Jackson, a resident and close neighbour to the professor." At this point I saw Malcolm look up and over his glasses, straight towards me. I continued. "My question is for Professor McKenzie. I am presuming that if the power station is to be built, property values will decrease. Maybe for the short term, but in real cases of urgency, will the government be helping out any homeowners that have to move?"

I sat back down. I cannot remember what answer Malcolm McKenzie gave. All I remember is his eyes looking straight into mine while he answered my question. I was so attracted to him. Sexual feelings were zapping through my body.

Once the meeting was over, Joyce insisted that I go for a drink with her. She told me that most of the men our age, single or married, frequented local bars—in particular the public house next to the town hall.

Joyce was so thorough as she made her way round the public house, making sure that she introduced me to everyone there. I had a wonderful night. There were many eligible men there. I recall giving my phone number to at least three men. One particular man, a farmer, caught my attention. He was very handsome, and he made me laugh—always a good starter for ten.

He introduced himself to me as Ben Wilcock. He told me that he owned and farmed all the land that surrounded my cottage. I presumed not only that he was a handsome, attractive man but also that he was quite a wealthy man. Ben Wilcock was a tall man of medium build, with blond hair and baby blue eyes. He was quite dishy. Although Ben Wilcock did not ask for my phone number, he knew exactly where I lived!

That night, I curled up in bed next to Brutus, and I recalled everything that had happened that night. I could not stop thinking about Professor Malcolm James McKenzie. I wondered about the woman he had been with. I knew I had to keep trying to meet the professor. I must admit that the professor did not seem to be very interested in me that night.

I thought to myself, *Early days yet! Yes, early days yet! No way am I going to give up on the wish that the professor and I will one day get together!*

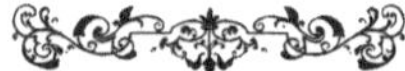

Every day, Professor Malcolm James McKenzie was in my thoughts.

I just did not know how I could get to meet him socially.

One morning, after I had seen his black car leave, I concocted a devious plan—or so I thought! It was late November and very cold. I put on my winter coat, and with all my best clothes on underneath the coat and in full make-up, I decided to watch out for the return of his car. As soon as I caught sight of his car returning, I pretended to be gardening in my small front garden.

As Malcolm James McKenzie pulled up outside his large gates, and while he was waiting for the gates to open, I made myself visible and shouted a hello, and to my pleasure, he looked across to return my greeting.

"Good morning, Miss Jackson. A beautiful day, is it not?" said Malcolm.

"Yes. It truly is. I have just made some coffee to warm myself up.

Would you care to join me?" I asked hopefully.

"Sorry. Maybe another time. I am running late today," replied Malcolm. Then he changed his mind and said, "Well, actually, yes, I think I will join you for a coffee."

My heart was pounding, my face was burning, and my hands were shaking as I entered my cottage and made my way to the kitchen and the coffee machine.

The coffee was good and hot, and I heard Malcolm enter through my front door.

"What a quaint cottage this is," said Malcolm as he caught his head more than once on the low beamed ceiling.

"I think, for your safety, we had better have the coffee in the back of the cottage, in the dining area. The ceilings are considerably higher in there,"

I said as I laughed. Malcolm also found the funny side and laughed with me.

For an hour, we talked, we laughed, and if I am not mistaken, we flirted. Our eyes seemed to lock together. I had never been so sexually aroused as that before. I only wished that Malcolm, found me as attractive as I found him!

I watched every movement he made. He was considerably older than I was—maybe in his mid-fifties. He was very tall, of medium build, and he seemed always to be so smartly dressed. He was quite baldish, but he looked so distinguished. At last I looked straight into his eyes. They were dark grey in colour. He seemed to be a very quiet, studious gentleman who had the knack of holding my attention by staring straight into my eyes. When he spoke, he spoke softly; he never raised his voice.

That hour that he was with me in my cottage went by so quickly. I insisted that he address me as Pauline, and he returned the gesture by asking me to call him Malcolm.

"Thank you, Pauline, for your hospitality. I have to go now! I am so far behind with my work, but it was a pleasure having coffee with you and looking around your cottage. It is beautiful. Very cosy!" said Malcolm as he left, banging his head at least twice. We both laughed.

I would have given anything for one more hour in his eyes! I could not keep jumping out of my front garden to get Malcolm's attention. What else could I do? I had no idea at all.

Over the next few weeks—and, indeed, over the Christmas period—Joyce Macey visited me quite often. She invited me to visit her bungalow, which I did on several occasions; and before long, we were both very good friends.

We socialised quite well together. We had most things in common, and life had treated her with so much similarity to the way life had treated me.

We frequented cinemas, restaurants, social events, and, of course, the pub. Both of us enjoyed nights in together. With good food and plenty of wine, we used to talk and laugh for hours. Either I would sleep at hers or she would sleep at mine.

Joyce had one goal in her life, and that was to meet and fall in love with a man she could marry and settle down with. She had met many men, but all she managed were broken relationships and heartache. Joyce was still looking.

I had no interest in falling in love and settling down with any man. I was far happier on my own with my trusted dog, Brutus. I had never discussed Malcolm with Joyce. She was not aware that I was falling in love with him though I did not even know him. I never went a day without thinking of him, and these thoughts of him sent shivers all through my body. I had no control over the way I felt about him. I believe they call this unrequited love. That is, love that is one-sided and is usually unknown to the other party.

One evening in with Joyce at my cottage—a drunken evening in—we discussed Joyce being totally unhappy with her lot at her post office. Joyce was tied to her post office day after day. She was seriously thinking about selling up, releasing the capital and doing things that she had always wanted to do. For example, she said that she wished to travel. There was one major flaw to that plan, and that was that she would have no income at a later date.

Before the end of our drunken night in, I agreed to purchase 50 per cent of her post office and take over 50 per cent of the work and responsibilities that went with the post office. That would provide Joyce with some capital, and it would give me an investment and some work that would give me an income. Joyce was thrilled with the proposition and relished the thought of not being tied to the post office during every working hour.

The following morning, both of us were suffering from hangovers, but we were both in the same mind as to our agreed business arrangement. Joyce left my cottage all excited, and she said she would contact her solicitor straight away. I was to turn up at the post office on the Monday morning for my first induction. Joyce was not the only one all excited; I could hardly believe my luck!

Monday morning, bright and early, I made my way to the post office. The morning went by so fast as Joyce showed me all the ins and outs of managing the post office.

As I was about to leave, I noticed tickets for sale for the New Year's Eve celebrations at the town hall. I was just about to mention to Joyce that we should go to it when Joyce said, "That should be a good night—a dinner dance with a complete band for the evening's entertainment. Even Professor Malcolm McKenzie has purchased four tickets!"

That was it! I had to go! "Right, Joyce, I think we should go and let the new year in properly. It's a new era for the both of us!" I screeched with excitement.

Joyce agreed, and we both laughed at my excitement. If only Joyce knew why I just had to be there. I just wanted one chance to find out if Malcolm might be interested in me!

The Christmas period in the town was magical. I was so looking forward to seeing Malcolm again. Apart from a wave from his car every now and again, I had not been able to get any contact with him.

I took delight in having my hair done and of course purchasing a most beautiful, elegant evening dress. I had always suited the colour pale green, so I made sure that I chose an evening dress in that colour. Even if I said it to myself, I looked good!

New Year's Eve came at last. The taxi arrived, and I joined Joyce in it. We were like two very young women, laughing all the way to the town hall.

I recognised so many people from the town. I danced with quite a few men. I danced and laughed with Ben Wilcock, the farmer I had previously met. He was charming and a pleasure to be with. All the while, I was looking around the large room, trying to see if Malcolm was there.

At last I spotted the table he had been seated at. He was accompanying several men and women. He seemed to be constantly in the company of the woman I had seen in his car many times.

"Joyce, do you know of the woman who is with Professor McKenzie?" I asked Joyce, sort of matter-of-factly.

"No, sorry! I have seen her many times with him. She sometimes comes into the post office with him. Why?" replied Joyce.

"No reason," I added.

After the meal, the band set themselves up on the stage, and they took over the rest of the nightly entertainment. They were brilliant.

I glanced across the room to where Malcolm was seated, and to my pleasure, Malcolm was looking straight back at me. Looking directly into his eyes, I smiled, and to my amazement, Malcolm winked at me! I smiled coyly and nodded. He returned my smile.

The drink was flowing, the music was good and very loud, and the atmosphere was electrifying. I danced with Ben, and I danced the stupid dances with Joyce. All the while, I was trying to get together a plan that would result in me dancing with Malcolm. No such luck. In the end, I made my way to the bar to purchase a good, long, cold lemonade. Within seconds, I was standing next to Malcolm, who had also made his way to the bar to purchase drinks.

"Fancy meeting you here!" laughed Malcolm. "Oh, that is so cheesy!" I replied, laughing.

"The band is very good!" said Malcolm, trying to make conversation.

"Will you dance with me, Malcolm?" What the hell was I playing at? I was mortified that I had asked him to dance with me.

"Of course, Pauline, but I must warn you that I cannot dance. While everyone was learning to dance, I must have been doing something else."

As we made our way to the dance floor, I said, "Hold on to me, and short, small, slow movements always works for me!" We both laughed.

As Malcolm and I held each other on the dance floor, there was no need of any conversation. I loved the feel of him holding me. Malcolm pulled me closer and closer to his body. Our cheeks were touching, and so were the rest of our bodies. I could feel his manhood, erect and throbbing, pressed up against me hard. Our lips touched gently, and we moved slowly to the music.

"Right. Ladies and gentlemen—your attention please," said the compére. "Five minutes to go before we let the new year in!"

Malcolm released his hold of me and apologised to me before making his way back to his table and his party. *What the hell happened there? I* thought to myself. *Why did he apologise?* I was so in love with him, and now I knew that he was just as attracted to me as I was to him.

The new year was upon us, and everyone was hugging and kissing. I felt so low! I did not want to be mauled and kissed by all and sundry! I made my way outside and walked away from the door I was looking up at the stars when Malcolm came and stood by my side.

"Happy New Year, Pauline," Malcolm said, and at the same time he pulled me close to him, and we kissed each other passionately. What a kiss that was!

"Happy New Year, Malcolm," I said as he was walking away . "Can I call on you in the future?" asked Malcolm.

"I would be so disappointend if you didn't." I replied We both laughed.

That night, when I returned home to Brutus, I was still confused about what I should do about Malcolm. I knew I was totally in love with Malcolm, and I knew he was not in a serious relationship with his woman friend. How could Malcolm be in a serious relationship with his woman friend if she was kissing another woman so passionately?

Brutus was jumping all over the place, excited about the walk he was expecting. I placed his collar over his neck, and off we went, walking down the lane towards the end of the lane itself. As we turned the corner towards the end of the lane, I removed Brutus's lead. I knew there would be no passing traffic, so it was very safe for Brutus to run free.

We carried on walking, and my thoughts were with Malcolm. Oh, if only Malcolm could fall for me! I turned to place Brutus's lead back on, and to my horror, Brutus was nowhere to be seen!

CHAPTER 6

Unrequited Love

A FEW WEEKS INTO THE New Year, Malcolm had not been in touch. I had not seen his car coming and going. I presumed that he was working away.

All the legal papers had been completed on my buy-in of the post office, and I was working in the post office parttime. Joyce and I made the perfect team, and our friendship blossomed.

One lunchtime, I was serving at the counter, and I asked for the next customer. I looked up, and there standing in front of my counter was Malcolm.

"Oh, good day, Malcolm. I have not seen you of late.

What can I do for you?" I asked professionally.

"Good day, Pauline. Can you send these letters for me? First class. Thank you!" said Malcolm, then he touched the peak of his cap and bade me good day.

I looked out of the window and saw the woman he was always with standing next to him, and then they walked away. I thought to myself, *What is the matter with me? Why does he not find me as attractive as I find him? I know he enjoyed kissing me on New Year's Eve. Perhaps he has a close relationship with the woman I always see him with. Perhaps I seem too needy. I will step back a little, and when I do bump into him, I will try to seem more aloof. Yes, more aloof!*

That night, Joyce and I had arrangements to meet in the pub. I was early, so I made myself comfortable in a small, snug room. Within five minutes of me sitting down, in walked my friend Ben Wilcock.

We had a drink, and we talked and laughed. I found Ben extremely attractive. If it had not been for my feelings for Malcolm, I would probably have gone out with Ben, become his lover, and married him. I did agree to go out with him the following weekend, and I was excited at the prospect.

It was a pleasant night. All my friends were laughing and, in some cases, singing. I arranged a time and date with Ben, for our night out, and as I was about to leave, I glanced to the back of the main room. There in the shadows of the fire I saw Malcolm's lady friend passionately kissing another person. I looked on with amazement when I realised that the other person was in fact a woman!

I knew that it was nothing at all to do with me. "Live and let live" was my motto, but I did wonder if Malcolm knew of the situation and whether he would look more favourably towards me if he did.

As I left the pub, Ben grabbed me and flung me around. His lips were on mine, and he kissed me very gently. I must admit that I did enjoy that kiss, which made me feel better at the prospect of dating Ben.

"Brutus! Here, boy! This way, Brutus! Brutus! Here boy!" There was no sign of him! I began to panic. For at least fifteen minutes, I called and called for Brutus.

I stood there listening to the silence. Darkness had fallen, and the moon was up, shining ever so brightly. I frantically looked around, trying to see my beloved dog, Brutus. Nothing! Where was he? What was I to do now? I could and would not return home without him. I considered that he had perhaps returned home on his own. If he had, I was bound to chastise him for frightening me so!

As I turned to walk back to my cottage, hoping that Brutus was already there, I thought I heard him whimper. I frantically looked around in the moonlight, all the while shouting his name. Then I saw him! He was on the other side of the tall wire fence that surrounded that part of the Formby estate.

Brutus was running to and fro along the wire fence, and he was getting distressed. I was also distressed as I walked up and down the wire fence, trying to find where Brutus had made his entrance into Malcolm's estate.

"Here, Brutus. There's a good lad. Show me where you got through the fence," I whispered softly. Brutus kept running back and forth, trying to get to me. I fell towards the fence and realised that I had found a small opening under it. I dug away with my hands until I had prepared a hole big enough for me to get Brutus through it. Brutus was having none of it! He would not come to me through that hole in the fence. There was only one thing I could do, and that was dig some more earth away and climb through to Brutus.

At last I was through, and every time I tried to put his lead on, he ran further away from me. He seemed very frightened. I kept talking to him, very softly, trying to reassure him. Eventually I managed to put his lead on, and I sat and cried with relief.

I stood up and looked around. I seemed to be in the middle of the woods. I could not see the wire fence. Before I could start to worry, I heard dogs growling and barking. Brutus was pulling on his lead, frantically trying to run away. Then I saw them—two Dobermann pinschers. They were creeping up on us, growling and snarling. I could see their large teeth. Brutus was going berserk, but I held on tightly to his lead. I held my ground, not daring to take my eyes off those large, vicious dogs.

It all happened so quickly. I saw them running towards us, and I threw myself on top of Brutus, who was screaming and trying to get away from me, but I held on tightly. The dogs were on us in seconds. I lay there on the ground, on top of Brutus. I was screaming for someone to help us. I felt pain in my arm, and I knew my forehead was bleeding. Someone whistled, and the dogs ran away. Not only did the dogs run away, but Brutus, who was still screaming, broke free and disappeared into the night.

I got up from the ground and tried to give chase to Brutus, but I did not see which way he had run. My legs were like jelly, and I fell hard to the ground again. Then I was physically sick.

"You stupid bitch! What do you not fucking understand about 'No Trespassing'!" someone shouted. I turned, but I could not make out who it was. At first I thought it might be a gamekeeper or someone similar, but then I recognised Malcolm.

"How dare you! Your perimeter fence had been breached, and my dog ended up on your property. I could not leave him to the mercy of your bloodthirsty hounds! You lock those dogs away until I find my dog! Do you hear me, you buffoon!"

"For goodness' sake, Pauline, he is a fucking dog. He will find his way home come what may!" continued Malcolm, still shouting.

"My dog is now trapped on your estate with no way of leaving to find his way home! Do you think he will ask you to open the gates for him—if he ever finds his way back to them? You lock those dogs of yours away until my dog is safely back home with me. Do you hear me? I said *do you hear me?*"

I turned and started to walk in the direction in which I thought Brutus had run.

"Where the hell are you going now?" shouted Malcolm.

"I am going to find my dog and bring him home. He was terrified, and I do not know if he was injured," I said.

"You stupid bitch! You cannot walk these woods at night! You look as if you have been hurt. Come here! Do not walk away from me!" shouted Malcolm.

I was furious with Malcolm. I hated his attitude, and I was worried for the safety of my dog, Brutus.

It was at this point, that I fell hard again onto the ground. By this time Malcolm had caught up with me, and as he tried to help me up, we fought. I tried to lose his hold, but Malcolm was stronger than I was. He was holding me so close. Even though I was so worried for Brutus, I could still feel those delicious feelings raging through me. I could feel Malcolm's breath against my face. I looked up into his eyes. They were cold. There were no feelings in his eyes. I just gave in. I was feeling very rough and very sick.

Malcolm was pushing me towards the large house. He was still holding tight of me, and then I was sick all over him. I laughed! I actually laughed! Then I cried.

We walked into the rear of the building and straight into the kitchen. What a mess I was. I had mud, sick, and blood all over me, and of course there was mud, sick, and blood on Malcolm.

As Malcolm started to take my coat off, he shouted to the woman.

"Amy, you have to take this woman to the hospital! She will need stitches to her arm and probably a tetanus injection. There is no way I want an ambulance coming here. Take her now! I have to finish my work, and I have been drinking."

"Malcolm, please lock your dogs away until I come back to find Brutus." I said quietly.

"You are not coming back here tonight!" said Malcolm.

"Do not tell me what to do! I will be coming back here, and I will find my dog!"

"Please your fucking self. I have to work to finish a project. I am away first thing tomorrow morning." With that, Malcolm left the room.

The woman called Amy took me to the local hospital. We did not have too long to wait, and a few hours later, we were on our way back. My arm had been bitten by Malcolm's dogs, and I had needed quite a few stitches and a tetanus injection.

On the way back to the estate, I tried to make conversation with Amy. "I saw you tonight in the local pub. You were with a woman, and you were sat in the far corner of the large room," I said.

"Yes, we were in the pub tonight," answered Amy. "I presume that Malcolm does not know about your friendship with that woman?" I asked.

"What has it got to do with you, anyway? Malcolm is aware of my relationship and has never made any objection to it," said Amy. "Malcolm is a top British nuclear scientist. He travels the world. He works very hard, and I am there to take care of my brother. We love each other very much, so I respectfully ask you to stay out of our lives and keep your opinions to yourself!"

We both fell silent. How stupid had I been, for goodness' sake! "Amy, I am so sorry. I have been completely out of order. I thought that you and Malcolm were an item. Oh! I feel so embarrassed. Please do not tell Malcolm. He already thinks that I am a stupid bitch—his words."

Amy was not amused, so we continued our journey in silence.

When we returned to the house, the light from the moon had disappeared behind thick cloud. I could no longer see my way to finding Brutus.

"Please leave me at my cottage. Amy, please, please ask your brother to keep his dogs locked away until Brutus is found. I need to get access to the grounds very early tomorrow morning. How do I do that?" I asked.

"Malcolm will be leaving for the airport very early. I will leave the gates unlocked for you. Will that be all right?" asked Amy.

"Thank you, I am most grateful. I am so afraid that I will never see my dog Brutus again. I love that dog so much. He has been a lifesaver to me. I owe him such a lot.

I am not going to let him down now!" I whispered.

"I hope you do find your dog and that he is not injured. Here, make a note of my telephone number, and please let me know if you find him," said Amy.

As soon as I realised Amy was no longer annoyed with me, I took the opportunity to ask her, very tactfully, if her brother Malcolm was in a relationship. She told me that it had been a very long time since Malcolm had been in a relationship with a woman. He was always working, and he did not seem interested in any woman.

Even though he had treated me badly that night, I knew I loved him. If anyone else had treated me like he had, I would never have wanted anything more to do with him.

I sat in my cottage, waiting for dawn to break. I could not sleep, and I could not eat anything. As soon as it was light enough, I set off through the Formby estate. All day I walked the estate. I shouted Brutus's name again and again. I stayed there until it was night again and too dark to continue my search.

I returned to my cottage. I tried to undress and wash my bloody and dirty hair, but I found it too difficult and painful with my arm stitched and bandaged. I was frantic that I could not find Brutus. As soon as dawn broke, I was back in the estate, walking and shouting for Brutus. There was no sign of him anywhere.

By early evening, I just had to give up. As I made my way back to my cottage, I received a phone call from Ben Wilcock. He wanted to know if I wanted to go out with him for a meal anytime soon. I told him my story and asked him to keep a lookout on his land for any sign of my dog. He said he would.

Defeated, I made my way back home. I managed to light the fire, and I just sat there wondering what I could do next.

Someone knocked at my front door. It was Ben Wilcock.

"Good God, Pauline! You look a complete mess! I presume you have not slept or eaten these past two days? What is that blood on you and in your hair? Are you injured?"

I could not answer him, as I was ready to cry and knew that if I started to cry, I would not be able to stop.

As the fire roared to life, Ben made me some scrambled eggs and a hot drink of sweet tea. I still could not talk to him, as I was so fretful.

Ben ran upstairs and ran a bath for me. When it was ready, he came downstairs.

"Come on, lady," said Ben. "A hot bath will make you feel better! I will help you undress to make sure you treat that injury with respect."

"Sorry, Ben. The last thing you should be doing is taking care of me. I am capable of undressing, and yes, I need a bath to relax in and to wash my hair in."

"Right! Come on, then! Go upstairs, and I will be helping you undress; and yes, I will be helping you bathe—especially washing your hair. There is quite a lot of dried blood in the back of your hair! Don't be awkward. I don't see anyone else here offering to help you. I think we should make this experience a pleasurable experience. What do you think, Pauline?"

I just laughed nervously. Ben also laughed nervously.

"Okay, Mr. Farmer; do your worst!" I said, and then I laughed again.

When I walked into the bathroom, I could see the bath was a massive bubble bath. At least my modesty would be protected. I could not see beneath the bubbles.

Ben slowly helped me undress, taking much care so he would not hurt my injured arm. He was quite naughty, as now and again his hands touched my breasts and nipples. When I was left with just my knickers on, I told him to turn away, as I was capable of taking my own knickers off.

Naked, I slowly lowered myself into the hot bubble bath. I lay back and then told Ben that I was ready for him to wash my hair. I had to leave my poorly bandaged arm hanging out over the side of the bath.

Ben took his shirt off and winked at me. "Well, you don't want me to get my shirt wet, do you?" he said with a cheeky grin. He knelt at the side of the bath, and without any hesitation, he began to stroke my breasts under the bubbles. It was a very pleasant feeling, so I just lay there and watched him. I must admit, he did make me smile. He moved from the breasts to the nipples, and then he stroked me all over my body. We both laughed as he stroked my clitoris, and then he stroked me between my legs.

"Right! Now that you are relaxed, I will wash your hair—unless, of course, you wish me to continue feeling you?" said a cheeky Ben.

"Thank you, Ben. As pleasant as that was, I am desperate to have my hair washed," I replied.

"Your wish is my command! Are you sure you don't want me to continue feeling you?" asked Ben. We both laughed.

When Ben had finished helping me, he held a bath towel up for me so I could wrap myself in it.

"Wrap this small towel around your hair and head. You don't want to wet your pillow, do you?" asked Ben.

"No, I will be all right. It will dry as I sit up in bed," I replied.

"Sorry, Pauline, but you will not be sitting up in bed; you will be lying down in bed, next to me. Is that understood?" asked Ben as he smiled and winked at me.

"Understood, Mr. Ben Wilcock!" I replied.

I threw my wet towel away as Ben took off all his clothes. What followed next was the most pleasurable, exciting, slow intercourse. Ben was not a selfish lover. He made sure that I climaxed before he climaxed. We both fell asleep in each other's arms. I was so tired, and the next thing I remember is Ben whispering that, like all other farmers, he had to leave and start work early on the farm. Then I heard him leave.

I woke to the sound of my phone. I answered it, and to my surprise, it was Ben. It was only six o clock, and I thought he had only just left.

"Well, my beautiful Pauline. Today is your day! Guess who I found in my barn? He is whimpering and he needs his mum. We are on our way!" shouted an excited Ben.

I screamed with delight. I hurriedly dressed as best I could and ran downstairs. Ben had stoked my fire and built it up for me. What a guy!

By the time I opened my front door, Ben was pulling up outside the cottage. In bounded Brutus. I fell to the floor with him in my arms. I cried with relief and delight. Brutus was still whimpering and licking my tears away.

"How will I ever thank you?" I asked Ben.

"Yes, I was good, but you don't need to thank me. I enjoyed the sex just as much as you did!" said a cheeky Ben. "Make sure you only feed him small meals for a while. He might not have eaten for at least a couple of days." With that said, Ben left.

Brutus and I lay on the rug in front of the fire for I don't know how long. I examined him, and I could see no injuries. I sponged him down with warm water to clean his muddy fur, and as Ben had suggested, I fed him small meals.

When Brutus was asleep in his basket, I took great delight in phoning certain friends of mine to tell them the good news. When I spoke to Amy, she was so pleased for me, and she said she would phone her brother, Malcolm, to tell him that Brutus had been found.

Although Ben had been there for me and had even made love to me, there was only Malcolm who made my heart race and made me feels so senxually excited. I knew I was in love with Malcolm, but there was little chance of him ever knowing or loving me in return. To hell with unrequited love; I wanted true love. I wanted Malcolm to love me back!

Joyce was so pleased that Brutus and I were reunited.

She was concerned that I had had a tremendous shock.

"Pauline, why don't you take Brutus with you on a trip to visit your cousin Emma in France? You could make it an extended holiday. I will see to the post office until you return. Then I can go off on an extended holiday while you take care of the post office."

"What a good idea, Joyce. I am already on it!" I said, laughing.

Within two days, I had updated Brutus's passport at the vet and had booked my train on the Euro Tunnel. I asked the local garage to check my car, and I packed my things and Brutus's things. Emma and Jeff were thrilled when I contacted them and asked if I could join them for a few weeks.

Brutus and I set off the following day. The journey was easy. Brutus made the whole experience enjoyable. Before long, we were driving south through France. We had to take a hotel for one night, and even that was enjoyable because I had Brutus as my companion.

At last we arrived at Emma's French cottage. I enjoyed every day there. We had good weather, good food, good wine, and good company. I made new acquaintances with both men and women. Every day, I would walk Brutus along the beach and we would call at the local beach bars for a drink or two. Every day was a joy.

Ben Wilcock phoned me several times, and we would talk and laugh together. Ben was a huge flirt. I knew that he had several women on the go at the same time, but that was how Ben was. What a guy! He was not the marrying kind, but as a true friend and lover, he was superb!

I received one phone call from Professor Malcolm James McKenzie, and that was for him to tell me he was relieved that Brutus had been found and that he had not been found on his land.

Malcolm seemed a very selfish man; even so, I was determined to get to know him better.

"Malcolm, when I return home, I would like you to come to my cottage, and I would like to cook you a meal to thank you for helping me that awful night," I said, lying through my teeth. He had never helped me and Brutus. He probably never gave us a second thought, but it was an excuse to get Malcolm to come to my cottage. Malcolm thanked me for the invitation and agreed to come, and he said he would look forward to it!

All too soon, it was time for Brutus and me to make the return journey. We had both enjoyed every minute with Emma and Jeff. It did cross my mind that, because I knew everywhere in that region by then, I would probably buy a small place there for myself one day.

Before long, we were back at home. I lit the fire, unpacked the car and prepared a beef casserole in the oven. My next job was to take Brutus on his walk.

On our way back, Malcolm was driving up to his gates. He stopped to talk to me. I was so pleased that I looked good and heathy with a rich tan and had some beautiful clothes on and had my hair beautifully tied back. We chatted, and then I suddenly asked him if he was interested in a rich beef casserole, a bottle of wine, and some good company. Surprisingly, he accepted my invitation. He parked his car across the road and came straight into the cottage.

I quickly arranged my clothing and combed my hair. I had been travelling all day, so I did not look my best. *Why did I invite Malcolm to my beef stew and wine when I am obviously not looking my best? Why do I always invite Malcolm on impulse?* I thought.

I told Malcolm to make himself at home, which he did, taking his cap and coat off and sitting himself down in the large chair by the roaring fire.

I continued in the kitchen, preparing the meal, and I gave Malcom the bottle of wine, the opener, and two wine glasses.

From the time he arrived at my cottage, we never stopped talking and laughing. The atmosphere was casual and wonderful.

I gave myself and Malcolm trays so we could eat the meal by the fire. I was proud of my beef stew—one of the best I had ever made. We drank the bottle of wine, and I replaced it with a second, and then a third. I loved his company. We both seemed to appreciate the same things. I loved Malcolm's smile and his laugh. I was so attracted to him.

I had drunk quite a considerable amount of wine, and that is all I remember of that night. I was so tired, as I had been driving all day; I must have fallen asleep—probably with the help of all that wine.

I woke up in the early hours of the morning. I had been asleep on my sofa in the lounge, and I had a coat over me. I presume Malcolm placed the coat over me before he left. He had also placed the fireguard around the fire.

I was so embarrassed at my behaviour! Had I fallen asleep and then started to snore? Or worse still, had I slept with my mouth wide open, maybe slavering? Oh, I was so upset with myself!

I had no telephone number for Malcolm; otherwise, I would have called him the following morning to apologise for my unseemly behaviour.

It was a few days later, while working at the post office, that I met Malcolm again. As he stood in front of me at the post office counter, asking me to weigh his letter post, I tried to apologise for that infamous night, but before I could start my conversation—the one I had rehearsed a thousand times—Malcolm said, "Good morning, Pauline.

I really enjoyed our dinner the other night. Good food, good wine, and good company. I would like to do it again, if it is all right with you. I will give you a tour of Formby House, followed by dinner."

The post office had suddenly become very busy, and there were customers queuing, so all I could do was say a feeble "Yes, thank you." Then Malcolm left without making definite arrangements.

I did not see Malcolm or his car for many weeks. I continued with my social life as before. Joyce and I had dinner with each other many times. Ben was becoming a frequent guest at my cottage. I treated him as a good friend, and I loved his company. He made me laugh, and he made me feel good. Ben used to say things like, "Are you ready for a bath yet? Do you want me to help you wash your hair? Can I wash your back when you have a shower? Do you want me to make you feel good tonight?" He whispered these short naughty sentences to me when we were in company, mainly in the pub. We would giggle like younger people. We had a lovely secret, which I knew Ben would never tell of.

When Ben offered to take me out to the cinema or for a meal and the like, I would go, and I would enjoy the so-called date with him. I made it very clear to Ben that I was not ready for a relationship—especially a sexual relationship—even though we had slept together. Ben was fine with that, but he insisted he wouldn't wait forever before he had a second chance of bathing me and then, in his words, fucking me. I would laugh, and he would laugh. I was always excited by his attitude. He was always smiling.

It was late summer, and Ben had arranged to take me to a restaurant in town. It was a meal booked for many farmers and their plus-ones. I had a lovely dress and jacket on—floral autumn colours—and I had had my hair cut short. When I put my make-up on and my jewellery on, I must say, I thought I looked brilliant!

As Ben turned up outside my cottage to pick me up, I came out of the cottage and started to lock my front door. Then I saw Malcolm walking through his open gates.

As usual, I acted on impulse. My heart was pounding, and I was so excited to see Malcolm. I turned to Ben and said, "I am so sorry, Ben, but I made arrangements to have a tour of Formby House and Estate with Professor Malcolm McKenzie. I really am sorry to cancel our date, but I can go anytime with you, though I might never get another chance to look over Formby House and Estate. I had totally forgotten about it!"

Ben looked disappointed but agreed that I should go to Formby House. He turned, and then Malcolm, who was by then walking across the road towards me, shouted, "Hello, Ben. I have not seen you for quite some time. How are you doing?"

I froze. What had I done?

"I am doing great! I did have a date with Pauline tonight, but it seems she prefers your company and is looking forward to you you showing her around Formby House. See you tomorrow, Pauline. Have a good night!" Ben then got into his car and left.

I just stood there. I could not believe that I had been so devious, but what was I to do now?

"So, Pauline! It seems you have used me to get out of going out with Farmer Ben. We must not miss the opportunity for me to show you my house, and you already saw the estate when you were searching for your dog. Fancy it? I can even offer you dinner and a few glasses of wine."

"Well, if you put it like that, I shall gracefully accept your offer."

We both laughed, and we started to walk up the long drive to his house. I was thrilled that Malcolm had invited me and that I was all dressed up. As we walked, we talked. I could see that Malcolm was looking at me intensely. I gently put my arm through his arm, and I hugged him as we walked along. He did not object to this; in fact, he squeezed my arm with his arm. I loved the delicious feelings that he gave me. I wanted him to feel as I did, and I hoped this would be the night that he showed me some sign of passion towards me.

We entered Formby House through the front door directly into a large hall. A large staircase wound round to reach the ground floor. Everywhere was painted white, apart from the black wrought-iron staircase. Beautiful pictures and paintings adorned all the walls. It was truly magnificent.

Malcolm took me from one room to another. The lounge was large but very cosy. The dining room was the same. When he took me into his laboratory, I was amazed. His laboratory ran the full length of his house, which seemed to be the whole of the left side of the house. All the other rooms were situated on the right side of the house. There was a downstairs cloak room, a small study and library, the kitchen, and, best of all, a music room.

I fell in love with the music room as soon as I saw it. There were large windows to the side and rear. It was all painted white with paintings on the walls, and the masterpiece was a large white grand piano.

I stood in the music room, and when I looked around it, I felt very emotional. I had never seen such a beautiful, calm room before.

"Come, Pauline. I promised you dinner, and dinner you shall have. I will open a bottle of wine, so come and make yourself comfortable in the lounge. My housekeeper, a Mrs. Roberts, comes in every day to clean and cook for me, and every night she leaves me a meal in the oven. All I have to do is turn the oven on according to Mrs. Robert's written instructions. I have no idea what the food is, but be assured it will be very good."

We sat in the lounge and we drank the wine, and when ready, Malcolm dished out the meal, which happened to be a cheese and potato pie.

While enjoying the meal, we talked and we laughed together.

We both seemed so at ease with each other's company. We got on so well together.

"I love your music room, Malcolm," I remarked.

"Good. Would you like to hear me play the piano? Playing the piano is one of my greatest enjoyments that I have. I am addicted to my piano, and I play for hours sometimes—especially if I have reached a complicated part in my physics. Sorry, I will not bore you with that!"

After we had finished our meal and drunk the best part of two bottles of wine, Malcolm took me into his music room, collecting some brandy on the way.

The piano seat was a long one. Its width was the same as the width of the piano, so when Malcolm told me to sit next to him at the piano itself, there was plenty of room for the both of us.

Malcolm could really play that piano! The sound was so clear and pronounced; listening to his music made me feel very emotional.

After a while, Malcolm stopped playing and we enjoyed a large glass of brandy each.

"Pauline, I am going to show you some basic piano notes to play," said Malcolm with a fire in his eyes that was burning me inside. Oh, how I loved that man!

We sat together on the piano seat, and Malcolm placed one of his arms around me and then held both my hands in his hands. I was so sexually excited, and the feeling of his hands around my hands only fuelled my feelings. He then helped me play a few notes.

"You are trembling, Pauline. Are you all right?" asked Malcolm. Stupid Malcolm! Could he not see what he was doing to me? Why did he not seem to feel the same way?

After another large brandy, it was time for me to leave. We walked back to my cottage arm in arm, laughing all the way. Malcolm made fun of my first attempt at a piano, and I laughed at him and his attitude to life.

When we arrived at the cottage, I undid my front door and I asked Malcolm if he would like to come in for coffee.

He gracefully refused and said he had some more work to do that night before he left on business the following day.

As Malcom said goodnight and turned to walk away, I just had to ask, "Are you not going to kiss me goodnight, Malcolm?"

"Err, Pauline, forgive me, but I am not looking for a relationship, and I am definitely not looking for a sexual relationship. I do not want you to get the wrong idea. I love your company, and I enjoy our time together. Good night, and thank you for a very enjoyable night." That said, he walked away.

"So does that mean you are not going to kiss me goodnight? Does that mean you will never kiss me?" I shouted after him.

Malcolm laughed and waved and carried on his journey back down his long drive.

I sat in my bed that night wondering if Malcolm would ever return my love for him. Why did I love him so much yet he seemed so cold when it came to passion for me? I went to sleep thinking of nothing but Malcolm. I remembered the truth about unrequited love. Unrequited love can make you feel depressed. It can make you feel physically ill—a worthless feeling. What was I to do? All I wanted to do was to love Malcolm and for him to love me in return.

The following morning was a beautiful morning. I sat outside my back door on my bench. I promised myself I was not going to feel depressed about my situation. I walked over to my bird table, and suddenly, through my back gate, in walked Malcolm. Malcolm put his arms around me and pulled me towards him; his lips were heavy on mine. I put my arms around his shoulders and pulled him even closer to me. We kissed so passionately. I could feel his tongue on my lips. I could feel his tongue on my tongue. I could feel his manhood pressing hard against me. There was no doubt that we were both sexually excited.

Not a word was said by either of us. Malcolm let me go and left the same way he had come, and then I heard his car drive away.

I sat down on my bench and thought to myself, *I now know that Professor Malcolm James McKenzie is in love with me, just as I am in love with him. Watch this space!*

CHAPTER 7

Disappointment

I WAS HAPPY AND EXCITED at the prospect of Malcolm and me getting together, for all the right reasons. I had convinced myself that when Malcolm returned, he would be just as eager as I was to start a meaningful relationship.

As the weeks went by, I busied myself with working at the post office and enjoying my dog Brutus and going out with friends. I did not say anything to anyone, not even to Joyce, about my feelings for Malcolm and my hope that Malcolm was missing me as much as I was missing him.

The weeks soon became months. No one had been in or out of the Formby Estate—not that I had seen anyway. Then one day I noticed a black saloon car drive through the large gates into the drive leading to Formby House. I waited and watched, and a few hours later the black saloon car drove away, closing the gates behind it.

I thought I might take the opportunity to phone Amy just to voice my concern about a car I did not recognise entering the estate. I would tell her that I knew Malcolm was away and that I did not have a phone number for him and was just being a concerned neighbour.

To my horror, I found that Amy's phone number was no longer in use. I knew that even Amy had not been seen for many months, and now I had no contact numbers at all for either Amy or her brother Malcolm. I was feeling very uneasy about this situation.

Another month went by, and one day, on my return home from working at the post office, there across the road, in all its glory, was a large For Sale billboard. I was so shocked. What was I to do next? Why had Malcolm not phoned me to tell me of the sale? It was always good manners to tell your neighbours of such an event. Malcolm had phoned me when I lost Brutus, so he obviously had my phone number. Even if he had lost it, he could have contacted the post office I was part owner of. He knew I worked there and was a part owner.

That night, I could not sleep. Had I been kidding myself about what feelings Malcolm had for me?

The following morning, I phoned the estate agency that had placed the For Sale sign on the Formby estate. They could not give me any information. Only interested parties would receive any information, and they would be seriously vetted before any information was given out.

With no contact numbers and no other way of contacting Malcolm, I was heartbroken. I had obviously misread every emotion and feeling I thought Malcolm had for me. What a stupid, old, lonely fool I was.

I knew I had to start rebuilding my life all over again. I was relieved I had not confided in anyone about my feelings for Malcolm. I would have been a laughing stock by now!

I carried on living my life with the same routine as usual. I had finally come to terms with the fact that I had misread the situation. In my heart, I was hoping that I might see Malcolm one more time at the Formby Estate before he moved on. That was not to be. Within weeks, a Sold sign was displayed; and a few weeks later, the new owners moved in.

I had no interest in meeting the new owners. They kept to themselves, and like Malcolm, they were only ever seen entering and leaving the gated estate.

True to form, I contacted my cousin Emma and asked if I could stop with them for a while. I offered no explanation. I was too ashamed to offer an explanation as to why I needed to be with them.

Emma was thrilled that I wanted to visit them. They were to be in France for a few weeks and then, when winter was well underway they were to return home for the winter season. I told them I would love to spend their last few weeks in France with them.

As I had done many times before, I packed my things and Brutus's things, and off we drove to France. I was depressed and heartbroken, and I could not pull myself together. If only I had not fallen in love with Malcolm.

When Emma and Jeff were ready to return to England for the winter months, I made my way back home with Brutus.

The cottage looked bleak. As I unlocked the front door, I saw that the inside of the cottage had lost its charm. I no longer liked the cottage, and I no longer wanted the cottage. Nothing seemed to please me.

I turned on all the lights, and I lit the fire. I turned on the central heating, and when I was unpacked and Brutus and I were warm, I ran myself a hot bath.

As I lay there in the hot soapy water, someone called out to me. It was a man's voice.

"Hey, Pauline, is that you upstairs?"

I jumped out of the bath, put a robe on, and peeped out over the staircase. I must have left the front door unlocked.

"Who's there?" I shouted.

"Who the fuck do you think is here?" came the reply.

"Ben Wilcock! You have frightened the living daylights out of me!" I shouted back, and then I said, "Make yourself useful and make me a hot drink. I am really cold!"

"What is the magic word, and what did your last servant die of?" replied Ben.

I hurriedly dressed and made my way downstairs. Ben had not made me a hot drink, but he had poured us both a large brandy instead. It was lovely to see him. I was at ease in his company.

Ben chastised me for leaving my front door unlocked and for having a bath without him. We both giggled, talked, and drank most of the brandy. Ben made his excuses to leave, as like all farmers, he had to be up so early in the mornings. I was alone again!

As I lay in bed that night, I knew that I no longer wanted to be alone. I wanted to be needed, and I wanted to love and be loved in return. There was nothing wrong with wanting to be needed. Ben was just a good friend, but I knew that somewhere there must be a man for me. There was nothing there for me anymore. I needed to sell up and move far away to start my search for a partner who would love me as I wanted to be loved. I had never been loved—just used.

I decided that after the Christmas and New Year period, I would talk to Joyce and explain what I wanted to do. Then I would put my cottage on the market, and once it sold, I would relocate somewhere else—maybe the coast down in southern England. I had not ruled out relocating to France—somewhere near Cousin Emma. The world was my playground, and I intended to enjoy it all!

New Year's Eve was upon us. I had made an arrangement with Joyce to go to the local town hall for the New Year's dinner dance.

I was feeling so much better, mentally and physically. I was all dressed up, with a new haircut, and I was looking forward to the evening. I had treated myself to an expensive long silk evening dress. I always seemed to choose the colour pale green, but on this occasion I had chosen a shimmering dark blue.

A taxi collected me from the cottage, and then we made our way to the post office to collect Joyce. We were both laughing and joking with each other. Joyce was a wonderful friend. Joyce had many men friends and indeed went on many dates, and she had been known to have had several good sexual relationships, but she had never settled down with any one individual. Joyce always said that she had not met the right one so she was going to enjoy continuing looking for him!

The evening was a great success. The food was good, the entertainment was good, the company was good, and the dancing was exhilarating. I danced the night away with several different partners.

I made one deadly mistake! I did not realise that I was drinking too much. As I was eating a five-course meal and drinking good wine, I was not aware that I was indeed drinking too much.

When twelve o' clock arrived, we all welcomed in the new year.

There was plenty of singing and plenty of hugging and kissing.

I did not enjoy all the kissing and fondling from the men there, so I made a hasty retreat into the garden, where all the smokers went. I took a large glass of red wine with me, and I sat myself down in a quiet corner.

"What are you doing here all alone? Have you run out of stamina?" said a male voice.

I looked up, and there, standing to the side of me, was my tall, handsome friend Ben Wilcock.

"You have a cheek! I don't recall you asking me to dance with you tonight, and no, I have not run out of stamina!" I replied. "Come on and dance with me now!"

"No thank you, Pauline. I like my women reasonably sober so that I can enjoy them," retorted Ben.

"My, my Ben! You talk as if you consider yourself to be God's gift to any unsuspecting woman!" I scoffed.

"Carry on talking in that manner and I will leave you here, and then you will have to try to get yourself home—a task I know you are now incapable of doing, as you are too drunk!"

My memory about the following events is fuzzy. I vaguely remember the taxi home—but home was not my home, but rather Ben's farmhouse.

I was very drunk, but I was not sick drunk. When Ben carried me upstairs to put me in one of the bedrooms so I could sleep it off, I insisted that I sleep in Ben's room and that I sleep in Ben's bed, but I would only sleep in Ben's bed if he would cuddle me. I remember being most insistent. Eventually, I assume, Ben just gave up on me, took my evening dress off, threw me into his bed, and then just disappeared out of the bedroom.

During the night, I awoke needing to use a toilet. By this time I knew where I was, but I had no idea where the bathroom was.

I staggered onto the landing and shouted, "Ben! Sorry, I need your help! Where are you? I need the toilet. Where is the bloody toilet?"

"For fuck's sake, Pauline! It is a good job I don't have to be up early tomorrow!" said Ben as he grabbed my arm and took me to the bathroom. "Don't lock the door! I don't want to have to break the bathroom door down if you collapse in a drunken heap on the floor!"

I was feeling better, and I was ashamed at the way I had behaved towards Ben. He had always been a good friend to me. I had really shown myself up.

I came out of the bathroom feeling very ashamed and sheepish. "Where have you been sleeping?" I asked. "Have I taken your room?

I am sorry."

Before I could finish my sentence, Ben said, "Shut up! Keep your mouth shut! Get back to bed!"

Ben grabbed my arm and marched me back into his room. I turned quickly, put my arms around him and I kissed him. I kissed him so seductively that I surprised even myself. Ben was even more surprised.

That kiss was brilliant! It did not take Ben long to realise that I wanted him to make love to me. I had only a silk under slip and a pair of knickers on, and Ben had only a pair of underpants on. We both took our clothing off and fell into Ben's bed.

There was the smell of male sweat; the feel of his body, warm and hairy; the feel of his gentle touch all over my naked body; the sensuous and passionate kissing; the feel of his erect penis rubbing between my legs; and the ultimate feeling of his penetration. Ben had proved to me once before that he was not a selfish lover. He made love with precision, mainly to give me the pleasure he wanted me to have. That night, Ben had me in so many different positions. I achieved more than one orgasm, and Ben climaxed more than once. The aftermath was so sweet as we lay in each other's arms. Hot, contented, and sweaty, we fell asleep holding each other tight.

I was awakened abruptly by the sun shining through the open curtained windows. As I recalled the night with Ben, I was horrified and very embarrassed. I was on my own in his bed. I could hear Ben downstairs. I could see my clothes neatly folded on a chair in the corner of the bedroom. I noticed what a beautiful bedroom it was—nothing like I imagined a farmer's bedroom to be like. I hastily dressed and made my way to the bathroom. Boy, did I look a mess! I had no make-up with me. My hair was a disgrace, and I was wearing an evening dress! I had no idea where my shoes or bag were.

I slowly and quietly made my way down the stairs and through the hall. I even noticed how fantastic the hall looked. All was very tastefully decorated.

I opened the kitchen door and was greeted by a very excitable Ben. "Good morning!" said Ben.

I stood there looking around the modern, fully fitted kitchen and dining area.

"You have a beautiful house, Ben. Sorry, I don't know what to say! I need to go home as quickly as possible. Can you take me straight away? Poor Brutus needs to have his morning wee. He will be wondering where I am, and I need a shower and a change of clothes." I fell silent and just looked at Ben.

"Pauline, you are not going back to your cottage yet. I have cooked you a good breakfast. You will feel much better if you eat something. Now, look outside the kitchen window and tell me what you see!"

I walked over to the kitchen window, and there in the yard was Brutus, running and playing with the other dogs.

"I took your keys out of your bag and went and collected Brutus early this morning. So, you see, you don't have to go anywhere yet!"

"Wow, Ben! Look at me! I am dressed in an evening dress—"

Before I could finish my sentence, Ben said, "And you are aware that you have the scent of sex on you and you want a good bath to wash it away. Am I right? Last night's sex was worthy of a honeymoon. We were brilliant together, and even if I say it myself, I am very proud of my performance. Do you agree?" asked Ben.

I looked at him in amazement. He did not seem at all bothered or embarrassed by our sexual activities. I suppose farmers openly deal with all sorts of weird things animals do. Not that we are animals; it was just that I was uncomfortable looking at Ben and then remembering what we had done to each other that night.

"Pauline, do you agree?" repeated Ben. I just nodded as I felt my cheeks blushing.

"Come on and eat your breakfast! I want you to listen to me real good! Okay?" said Ben.

Again I nodded as I tried to eat something. I was not hungry at all, but I thought I would try to eat a little just to please Ben.

"Pauline, come and live with me here. Move in with me. We make a great couple, and I will do everything I can to make you happy."

I just stared at him. What was I to say? I was planning to move away and start a completely new life within weeks. I had not discussed this with anyone except my cousin Emma and her husband.

"Well, Ben! You definitely know how to surprise me! Your timing is not very good. In fact, it is unbelievably awful! I am suffering a hell of a hangover. I cannot think straight and I am sat here in front of you looking disgusting, in an evening dress!"

"Right! Let me explain some things to you. I would not expect you to help around the farm unless you wished to do. I have Julie, a housekeeper, who comes most days, to do all the housework and cleaning. I have all the top range of kitchen and laundry appliances. I just want you to move in and live with me! You could always rent your cottage out."

Again I just stared at Ben. Silence came down into the room.

"Ah! I know what I have not said, and that is that I am in love with you, Pauline. I have loved you for so long. What do you say?"

"Ben, this is such a big deal. I don't think I love you as you say you love me. I love you as a great, loving friend. You will have to let me think about this," I replied.

"Right!" said Ben as he jumped up and knelt before me. "Marry me, Pauline!"

"Whoa! Hold on, Ben! I am going home now. Take me home! Let me get myself sorted. I do not feel well, and I know I need to calm this atmosphere we have between us."

Ben stood up, got his car keys, and walked out, collecting Brutus from the yard and he waited for me to get into his Land Rover. Ben and I did not speak to each other again. When we arrived at the cottage, I got out of the Land Rover and let Brutus out, and then Ben drove away at speed.

As I entered my cottage, I felt so upset inside. I started to cry, even though I did not know what I was crying over. What I did know was that my heart and soul were still pining for Malcolm. How could I contemplate marrying somebody when my heart and soul were with somebody else?

I lit my fire and ran a good, hot bath. I lay there soaking in the hot, soapy bath water. Somebody knocked on my front door. I put a bathrobe on and went to investigate who the visitor was. I was half hoping that Ben had returned, but no such luck. It was Joyce, bearing wine and nibbles.

As Joyce entered the cottage, she could see that I was distraught. She sat me down and poured me a large glass of wine, even though I really did not want it, and then I told her about the proposition Ben had made to me.

"Goodness, Pauline. He is a tall, handsome, rich, gentleman farmer. I find him incredibly sexy. I have fancied Ben Wilcock for a long time, but he has never been into me. If I were you, I would accept him straight away. Life is too short to mess about. We only live once. I am so jealous of you. I have wanted Ben to look favourably towards me, and I was hoping that one day I might even settle down with him."

I could not tell Joyce about my unrequited love affair with Malcolm. How ironic was this situation? I was deeply in love with Malcolm, but he was not in love with me. Ben was totally in love with me, but I did not love Ben. Joyce was probably in love with Ben, but he did not love her!

After Joyce had left the cottage, I curled up in bed with Brutus. I knew I had to get far away from my life there. I was right to plan a new life elsewhere. It looked more than likely that I would relocate to France, near where Emma and her husband where living. Jeff, Emma's husband, had been semi-retired from the police force for a few years. He had recently made the decision to retire fully in a few months' time. Emma and Jeff had decided they were going to sell up in England and move permanently to France. They owned a cosy, large, beautiful house in France, and of course the weather in France was far better than in England.

After hearing the news that Jeff was going to retire and that Emma and Jeff were going to move to France, I knew I could relocate to France. I would buy a house, maybe an old house, so I could busy myself with a renovation project. I could picture in my mind what I really wanted in a house in France. I was excited, and I knew that I had outlived the cottage, my friends there, and the place itself. I had very few good memories from that place. I knew I had to leave.

I could not start the process of moving and relocating until Joyce had, had her three-week holiday. She had planned it months before New Year When Joyce went off on her jollies to Tenerife, I was to take full control of the running of the post office. That part I was really looking forward to. I made the decision not to tell anyone of my intended plans. I would wait until Joyce returned from her holiday; then and only then would I start the process of selling up.

At last the time came when Joyce was away, and I busied myself looking after the running of the post office. I was contented, happy, and looking forward to the future. Every night after work, I would walk Brutus along the small country lanes, and on some occasions, I would walk across Ben Wilcock's farmland. I particularly enjoyed walking through his meadow fields; they bordered my rear garden, so I found it easy to walk back home that way.

After the incident of losing Brutus in the Formby estate, Ben had given me permission to walk his land rather than take a chance of Brutus going astray again in an inaccessible area.

As I walked Brutus through Ben Wilcock's meadow fields, I talked to Brutus about all the wonderful changes I had planned for us both. I knew that it seemed stupid to talk to a dog, but I believed that Brutus understood everything I was saying. Now and again I thought about Ben. He was such a wonderful man, and yes, he was tall, handsome, strong, and sexy. I could feel my body shudder when I recalled what Ben and I had done to each other in the privacy of my bedroom and his bedroom. I shuddered with the thought of how Ben had pleasured me and the sexual pleasure I had felt. I had also pleasured Ben, and I hope I gave Ben good sexual pleasure. What a pity that I did not love Ben enough. Every day, I was living with Professor Malcolm James McKenzie in my heart, soul, and mind. Even though we had never got to know each other properly, I could remember the few kisses we had shared, and that was enough for me to know that after living a loveless marriage for all those years, I was never going to make the same mistakes again.

Since New Year's Day, I had not heard anything from Ben. Perhaps that was a good thing.

On the second week of me looking after and working at the post office, I was just about to lock up when I heard the sirens of fire engines. I could not see them, but a couple of police cars had passed, as well as an ambulance. I did not give them a second thought until I was driving down the country lane towards my cottage.

As I drove down the long, winding road, I could see pillars of smoke in the distance. I knew it was my cottage. I drove as fast as I could until I drove round the bend near my cottage. I was horrifiedat the scene of flames and destruction. And then I remembered that Brutus was in the cottage!

I stopped my car and ran past all the firemen. I was screaming and screaming that my dog was in the burning cottage. Nobody was listening to me. The flames roared, and then the roof collapsed upon itself. A fireman dragged me away towards an ambulance. He kept telling me to stay calm. I continued to scream that I needed to get to my dog. I collapsed into the arms of an ambulance worker. The whole of the cottage was ablaze. Brutus would not have stood a chance.

Someone put a blanket around me, and people were talking to me, trying to calm me down. I stood there looking at my burning cottage, and I cried with despair.

I glanced across the road towards the Formby Estate. People were congregating around, watching all the activity, and then I saw Ben Wilcock. Ben was leaning on his Range Rover, which was parked a little way past the entrance to the Formby Estate. He was watching me. He showed no emotion but just stared at me.

I ran across the road towards him.

"Ben! Brutus was in there!" I could not say anything else. I was not capable of saying anything else. I just screamed and cried! Ben did not even try to comfort me. His eyes were cold, and his attitude was cold towards me! I turned to walk back towards the ambulance. A police officer met me and asked whether I had anywhere to stay and whether had I a contact phone number so they could reach me the following day. Before I could answer, Ben shouted, "Miss. Jackson will be staying with me. Here is my card with contact numbers. If you don't need her now, I will take her to my home." The police officer nodded.

I slowly walked back to Ben's Range Rover. I could not bear to look at the cottage. By that time, it was completely burnt out. I had lost everything. I knew I was insured, but the loss of all my personal things and my beautiful Brutus could never be compensated. I was devastated, and I presume I was in shock.

"Get in!" shouted Ben as he held the door open for me.

I started to cry again. I was sobbing so much that my chest hurt. "For fuck's sake, stop your crying! Brutus is fine! He is in my barn. He is shaken up, but he is not hurt."

I screamed at Ben, "Say that again! Now! Why did you not tell me before? *Say that again*!"

Calmly, Ben said, "I found Brutus wandering on the lane, near the farm. I put him in the Rover and took him to the farm. I have tied him up in the barn. It was only when I set off driving down the lane again that I realised smoke was to be seen on the horizon. As I neared your cottage, I could see all the flames. I called the fire brigade. The rest is history."

As we parked at the farm, I jumped out of the Rover and ran around to the back and into the yard. I ran into the first barn. There was no Brutus! I ran towards the second barn. I opened the barn door and ran inside. There was no Brutus there either! By this time, Ben had walked into the yard.

"Is this some kind of sadistic joke?" I screamed at Ben.

"I don't know, is it?" replied Ben. "You have a smaller barn to try yet, and then I will expect an apology from you!"

I ran to the small barn, and then I heard him whimpering and barking. I did not even open the doors to that barn. I just collapsed to the ground. I was shaking uncontrollably. I must have been in total shock. Ben opened the barn doors for me, and I got myself up and ran to Brutus. I hugged him and hugged him. I cried and I cried. I tried to undo the rope that was tied around his neck.

"Do not untie him! Leave him there until the morning. He is very spooked, and if you untie him, he will bolt and run," instructed Ben.

"No! I want him with me! I will never let go of him again!" I said while I tried to untie him.

Ben grabbed my arm and pulled me away from Brutus. He did not stop dragging me away until we were out of the barn. He closed the barn door and repeated, "Leave Brutus there until the morning. He needs to be on his own so he can compose himself. He is very spooked and needs to be kept quiet for a while."

Ben walked into the kitchen through the back door. I just stood there in the yard. I did not know what to do. I followed Ben towards the kitchen. Now that I knew Brutus was all right, I knew I could cope with anything—even Ben Wilcock on a very bad day!

"Don't expect to come in here until you have apologised to me!" said Ben as he blocked my entrance into the kitchen.

"I am sorry I doubted you. I should have known better!" I whispered.

Ben poured us each a large glass of brandy. He took a warm pie out of the oven and dished out two plates. I drank the brandy, but I could not face anything to eat.

Ben ate his pie and read his mail. He did not speak to me at all—not that I wanted him to. I was still sobbing, my chest hurt, and I had a massive headache.

"Pauline, you look a mess. Look in that mirror there!" said Ben.

I walked over to the mirror, and I was shocked to see myself all black and smoke damaged. I was a real mess. I was black, my hair was black, and my eyes were red and swollen.

"Go and have a shower. Do not lock the bathroom door. I will take your clothes and put them in the washer and dryer. They will be clean for tomorrow. You will have a busy day tomorrow sorting out your insurance and making reports to the police, et cetera.

I presume you have insurance?" I just nodded, and then I made my way upstairs to the bathroom. Ben collected my dirty clothes and left me one of his clean pyjama tops and a dressing gown.

"I have prepared a bedroom for you," moaned Ben. "I will bring you a sandwich and a hot drink. You will feel better tomorrow after a good night's sleep."

After the shower and a change into clean clothing, I made my way to the bedroom that Ben had prepared for me. He brought me a sandwich and a hot drink, and then he left, without saying anything. He closed the door behind himself.

I lay there most of the night, thinking. Weird! I thought. *Why did Ben not help me today? Why did he not tell me that Brutus was safe? Does he hate me so much that he wants to see me suffer? Oh, no! Did Ben have something to do with my cottage burning down? Somehow I truly believe he would be capable of such a thing. He knew that I would have to live with him at the farm if I had nowhere else to go. Until I sort out my insurance, I have nowhere else to go! I also have to run the post office. How could I ask Ben directly if he was involved with the cottage burning down? I needed Ben, and so did Brutus, so I must not accuse Ben of any misdoings."*

Eventually sleep came. Early the next morning, before Ben let his animal stock out to graze, he brought me a cup of sweet tea. But best of all, he brought me Brutus. I sat up in bed, holding onto Brutus and crying.

"Oh, for goodness' sake! Stop that fucking crying! I will be back in a couple of hours to make you and Brutus something to eat." Then Ben left.

All my clothes were clean and dry and folded on the chair next to my bed. I hugged Brutus for quite a while, and then I dressed myself. I made the bed and tidied my room, and then Brutus and I went downstairs to the kitchen.

I prepared the coffee machine and started the preparation for making Ben some scrambled eggs. I laid the table, buttered some bread, and then waited for Ben's return.

While I waited for Ben to return, I found my bag, and although my iPhone was running short on charge, I managed to find a contact number for the company who had insured my cottage.I had no other information for them—only the address of the cottage.

As Ben returned and walked into the kitchen, I walked over to him, placed my arms around him, and hugged him. I was surprised that Ben hugged me back.

"Fucking hell! Hugs, loves, and breakfast. Can't be bad!" whispered Ben into my ear.

That morning was manic! After finding an iPhone charger, the phone never stopped ringing. The local newspaper, the fire brigade, the police department, and the insurance company called. Ben had placed a notice in the post office window to state that the post office could not open on that Saturday morning, but normal working hours would resume on the Monday.

Ben's farm workers were good enough to come to the farm to do all the work that was required so that Ben could assist me with all the insurance claims and the like.

I had lost everything. I did not want to go and have a look at my burnt-out cottage. I had an appointment with the insurance claims person for Sunday morning, so that was the earliest I was able to view all the damage caused by the fire.

By late afternoon, all was sorted. I thanked Ben for all his help, and then I curled up on a sofa in the lounge with Brutus by my side and a roaring fire crackling away. I fell fast asleep.

"Right! Come on, Pauline. I will take you to the pub for a few drinks. It has been a bad day for you as well as for me. Are you coming?" asked Ben.

"No thank you!" I replied.

"Why not? It will do you good?" responded Ben.

I became quite fretful and angry. "Ben Wilcock, I thank you for all your help, but I have lost everything. I have no make-up, no change of clothes, not even a change of knickers, no perfume—no nothing. No! I do not want to go out for a drink. *You go!*" I shouted.

Ben did not need to be told that twice. I heard the front door close and his car pull away. Then, in the privacy of an empty farm house, I cried yet again.

By the time Ben returned, I had pulled myself together. He came in through the back kitchen door, bringing bottles of wine and a Chinese meal.

I could not be bothered to even talk to him, but I readily accepted the wine and the Chinese meal. I set the table in the kitchen, but I need not have bothered. Ben took his meal on a tray into the lounge and I sat on my own at the kitchen table.

When I had eaten, I cleared the kitchen table, poured myself a large glass of wine, and then made my way upstairs to my bedroom. I was cosy in that room. It was warm, had a beautiful outlook, and there was a television—not to mention that I also had Brutus to keep me company. That was all I needed for the time being.

I drank the full glass of wine, and then I heard Ben coming upstairs and going into his room. I could not sleep! I was still feeling very fretful, and I thought perhaps Ben would like some company in his room. All I really wanted was a cuddle, but with the way I was feeling, any attention at all was going to be welcome.

Dressed in Ben's pyjama top, I knocked on Ben's bedroom door. He did not answer, so I opened his door. Ben was sitting up in bed, reading. He looked over his reading glasses at me and said, "What do you want?"

"I feel so lost and insecure … any chance of a cuddle?" I said quietly. "Yep! But you are not getting in this bed with that top on. Take it off!"

"No! Forget it, Ben! You are determined to make me feel undermined. What the hell is the matter with you? Don't answer that; I really don't want to know. The sooner I am out of here, the better!" and with that said, I stormed out of Ben's room and returned to my room.

The following morning, the usual cup of hot sweet tea was brought to me. It had been arranged that I was to meet the insurance claims person at ten o'clock at the cottage. Ben had kindly agreed that he would accompany me. I was not looking forward to seeing the remains of the cottage. We drove to the cottage in Ben's Rover, and I took my bag, phone, and my car keys with me. I was to collect my car and return in it to the farm.

I would not get out of Ben's Range Rover. The insurance assessor joined Ben and me in the Rover, and within a short time, all the necessary forms and declarations had been completed.

As I left Ben's Range Rover, the claims assessor mentioned that I was entitled to be rehoused. I could be booked into a hotel or motel (with the dog) until such time as the insurance monies came through. How long it would be before the insurance monies came through was anybody's guess. He told me that he could arrange for me to have a large interim payment so I would be in a position to purchase all the things I needed—especially clothes, food, and the likes.

On hearing all that information, Ben drove away at speed back towards his farm.

I agreed to accept the interim payment, but I declined the offer of a hotel or motel room. I agreed with the assessor that Ben would be able to charge for putting me up and making sure that I was in a safe environment.

When the assessor had left and I was on my own, I slowly walked around the remains of my cottage. Somehow I did not feel that bothered, now that I had seen the result of the fire. One plus to all that had happened was that I did not need to put the cottage up for sale. The insurance monies would be paid out at market value, so all in all I was going to be better off.

Ben was my biggest problem. He had been so good to me and, of course, Brutus. Had he had anything to do with my cottage burning down? I had no idea, but I had my suspicions. I decided to stay on with Ben, and perhaps I would look favourably on remaining in that area. I doubted that, but I had to leave all my options open; after all, I was now officially homeless.

I returned to my car, and I drove straight to the nearest large town. There I found the largest department store that was open on a Sunday. I spent several hours purchasing all manner of goods, knickers, make-up, trousers, jumpers, coats, and hats—in fact everything I thought I would need over the following months.

I returned to Ben's farmhouse, and to my horror, I found the whole place in darkness. I was very tired, hungry, and cold.

I phoned Ben's number, and when Ben answered, I was livid. From the noises in the background, I knew he was in the pub.

"Well, Ben! Thanks a lot for locking me out. I am cold, tired, and hungry, and I am parked outside your front door with no way of getting in the farmhouse. If it was not so late, I would drive away and find somewhere else to stay."

"Are you still staying at the farm?" asked Ben. "Yes!" I replied. "Do you have a problem with that?"

"You mean you are not leaving the farm yet?" continued Ben.

"Yes. Again, do you have a problem with that—because if you have, I can make alternative arrangements for Brutus and me." I snarled those words at him. I was really pissed off by then.

"On my way! Don't go! Stay there!" shouted Ben down the phone.

As I waited for Ben to arrive, I placed all my shopping bags in the front porch so that I could collect them and carry them all upstairs to my room. I collected Brutus from the yard, and we both sat there in the front porch.

Soon Ben drove screeching into the drive and stopped next to my car.

As he got out of his car, he started to laugh.

"You look like orphan Annie with a dog!" shouted Ben. He was still laughing as he went to the back door to open up, and then, from the inside, he opened the front door.

"What the hell? Have you bought everything you have seen today? Why have you not moved into one of the hotels that that nice little insurance man told you about?"

"Get out of my way! I should have moved into one of those hotels, but I decided to torment you a little longer, okay?" I retorted.

"I am going to cut us both a large beefsteak, and I am going to cook us our evening meal. Wine, madam?" asked Ben.

"Plenty!" I replied, and then I carried all my purchases up to my bedroom. Even Brutus tried to help me, which was quite comical. For the first time in days, I enjoyed smiling.

I changed into a new tracksuit lounger—a bright blue-and-white one that fit me perfectly. All my old clothes that Ben had washed for me I discarded. With new slippers, a little make-up, and some perfume, I was beginning to feel like my old self.

Ben had previously spoken to Joyce and told her of my situation, but he had insisted I was more than capable of still running the post office. I spoke to Emma and Jeff so that they were aware of the awful happenings.

I quickly phoned Emma and Jeff and told them that everything was okay and that as soon as I could, I would be visiting them again.

"Come on, Annie! Your meal is ready; bring your dog!" shouted Ben.

As I walked into the kitchen, the look on Ben's face was a picture. He just stood there and stared at me.

"What?" I said.

"Nothing! No, you look beautiful. I would go as far as to say that you are the best looking woman that has sat at this table all year!" laughed Ben.

"Considering that we are only a few weeks into this year, that is quite a compliment, Ben" I replied.

That night, Ben and I had a wonderful, relaxing steak meal and plenty of wine. We laughed and we talked. I told him about all my purchases, and when Ben asked me if I had bought him anything, I replied "Yes!"

He was like a little boy waiting for a gift. He kept asking me to give him his present. I assured him that I had bought him something but that he would probably have to wait until the morning—until I had unpacked everything.

I was very tired, so after I cleared the kitchen, I said my goodnight and Brutus and I went to my room. I unpacked some of my purchases, and I smiled at the present I had bought for Ben.

For Ben I had purchased a pale blue basque, complete with suspenders, white stockings, and white-heeled shoes. I knew that it was a little risqué, but I needed some lighthearted fun. I also wanted to be held and cuddled. If sex was on offer, I was definitely going to take it. I really loved sex with Ben!

I prepared myself in the bathroom and placed Ben's pyjama top over the sexy outfit. I returned to my room and waited for Ben to retire to his room. It was ages before he retired.

I waited a little time, and then I knocked on his bedroom door. I opened his door, and as before, he was reading in his bed. He looked up over his reading glasses and said, "Not again! I have told you before—you do not get in my bed with that pyjama top on. It is up to you, but I promise you that if you remove that top, I will do my best to make you feel good and I will cuddle you all night, if that is what you so wish."

"Ask me where your present is?" I whispered. "Well, where is it?" asked Ben.

"Underneath this pyjama top!" I replied.

"I thought you said you had bought me something!" said Ben.

"I have. Promise me that you will only look and not touch," I whispered again.

Ben nodded, and then I removed the pyjama top stood there, and within seconds, Ben had flung me on the bed and we enjoyed the best sex that I had ever had. I know Ben enjoyed himself. It was wonderful!

We cuddled up together for the rest of the nigth. Just before we fell asleep, Ben whispered, "Pauline, you know that I love you, and I know you still have to realise that you love me just as much will never ask you to marry me again! If you want me, you will have to ask me to marry you. One day you will ask me to marry you! Don't leave it too late!"

CHAPTER 8

New Beginnings

DURING THE FOLLOWING FEW weeks, I lived at Ben Wilcock's farm. I enjoyed my bedroom. I was cosy, and I enjoyed living with Ben. Brutus always slept on my bed at night.
Ben took a great deal of pride in his farm. He worked long hours, and he worked hard. Julie, the housekeeper, was a very amiable woman, and we got on very well. I continued to work with Joyce at the post office, and Joyce and I continued to socialise together as we had done in the past.

There were occasions when I would slip into Ben's bed for a cuddle and some good sex. Ben never made any sexual advances towards me. It was always I who made the sexual advances towards Ben. Ben never refused my advances, and more than once he stated, "I will never again ask you to marry me. When the time is right for you, Pauline, and you realise that you are in love with me, it will be you who will have to ask me to marry you. Do you understand what I am saying? Do not leave it too late for you and me to start a life together. I know that we will be very happy together, but you have to work that out for yourself."

The insurance monies from the cottage were paid out pretty quickly. I insisted that Ben produce an invoice for the insurance company, billing me for my board and lodgings. Ben objected to the principle of charging me for living with him. at his farm, but I was most insistent that he was to receive monies he was rightly entitled to. We agreed on a compromise: whatever monies Ben received from my insurance company he would put to good use by way of starting a building project on the farm. He wanted to create a large building for use as a riding arena. Ben was determined to start a horse riding stable, and we spent many hours sitting in the lounge by the fire, planning for his new venture. Ben's farm had valuable space for individual stables for people to stable their own horses. He could provide as little or as much horse boarding as each customer would require.

Although I was happy and contented living at Ben's farm, I knew that I did not love Ben enough to commit my future to him and the farm. Every day, I thought about Professor Malcolm James McKenzie. The thought of him made me feel happy, sad, and confused, and I was determined that one day I would try to find him.

I knew that once I had received my insurance monies, there was nothing to keep me living at the farm. I knew that I should be honest with Ben and of course with Joyce. Ben and Joyce had been my saviours. I owed them both so much, but I was desperate to leave them and the area and start a new life somewhere else.

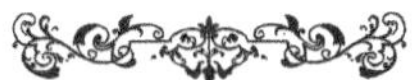

My cousin Emma's husband, Jeff, had finally retired fully from the police force, and they had sold their property in England and had moved permanently to their house in France. I was in constant touch with Emma and Jeff, and they knew that it was nearing the time when I would be joining them in France. I had plans to move to France and live with Emma and Jeff while I found myself a cottage that needed renovating. Such a project would give me something to do and would eventually lead to a new home for Brutus and me.

I was dreading telling Ben and Joyce about my plans. I needed to arrange for Joyce to either sell my share in the post office or maybe arrange to employ someone to work for her, and then maybe I would receive a return on my investment.

While I was working at the post office, I tried everything to see if I could find some forwarding address for Malcolm or his sister. The only postal record the post office had for Malcolm and his sister was that of a solicitor in London. Any mail for Malcolm was redirected to that solicitor's office. I tried phoning them and making plausible excuses as to why I needed a contact number for Malcolm and his sister, but they just insisted that if I sent them a letter they would forward it to Malcolm. So I did just that!

I wrote a short note to Malcolm. I told him that I was disappointed in the way he had moved away and that I was surprised he had not had the decency to let me know he was selling up and moving away. I told him I thought we were close and I hoped that in the future he would contact me.

I posted the letter to Malcolm's solicitor. I never received an acknowledgement or a reply.

My new passport arrived, and I took Brutus to the vet for his new passport. I had money in my bank, and I knew that I had to start to prepare plans for me leaving.

Wednesday was the day the post office was closed in the afternoon. I worked with Joyce on a particular Wednesday morning, and I told Joyce I was to go into the city and do some shopping. I asked her if she needed anything, and she replied that if I went into a certain department store, two pairs of silky grey stockings would be appreciated. I agreed to get the stockings for her, and then Joyce left. As I prepared to lock the post office up, I realised I could not find my purse.

I looked everywhere for my purse. I could only presume that I had left it in my bedroom at the farm. I needed my bank card from it, so, I locked the post office up and drove to the farm.

As I neared the farmhouse, I could see Joyce's car parked in the corner of the yard next to Ben's Land Rover.

I parked my car just outside the yard, and I walked into the farmhouse through the back door. Joyce and Ben were not in the kitchen. As I made my way upstairs to my bedroom to find my purse, I knew exactly where Ben and Joyce were!

I slowly and quietly walked up the stairs. I could hear the sounds of Ben and Joyce having sex. They were in Ben's bedroom. I was devastated! These two were my best friend and my so-called lover and friend.

I crept into my room, retrieved my purse, picked up my passport and Brutus's passport, and then crept downstairs and left through the back door. I collected Brutus from the yard and drove away. I was surprised at how hurt I was! I felt physically sick, and I could not erase the memory of the sounds that I had heard from Ben and Joyce having sex.

Joyce had always said that she thought Ben was wonderful and that she was quite jealous of my relationship with Ben. I had refused to settle down with Ben on more than one occasion, so what right did I have to feel so hurt and upset? I knew that I could never face Joyce and Ben again. I felt betrayed. I was jealous!

I drove to the post office, left Brutus in the car as I let myself in, and hurriedly collected all my belongings. I had nothing of any value, just a few clothes, such as a coat, a raincoat, and some personal papers. I wrote a note to my beautiful best friend Joyce.

When I leave, I shall lock the post office door and I shall post the keys through the letter box. I shall not be returning. It is the right time for me to leave.

I shall instruct my solicitor to handle all my affairs. Do not worry about the 50 per cent that I own of the post office and business. When the time is right for you, you may, if you wish, purchase the said same back from me. Do whatever you think is correct. Joyce, you are a wonderful woman. I am pleased that you chose to have me as a close friend and confidant. I will miss you terribly, but I know that I can no longer stay and be happy there with you and Ben. Say good bye to Ben for me.

Joyce, dream without fear and love without limits.

I am to go confidently in the direction of my dreams, and I am going to live my life as I want to.

Good bye, my beautiful friend. I wish you all the very best.

Out of my purse, I retrieved my solicitor's business card, and I placed it with my letter. I locked the post office door for the last time, and I posted the keys through the letter box.

I drove away, heading for the motorway that would take me south to the Euro Tunnel. I was breaking up inside. My best friend with my lover Ben. How long had that relationship been going on? Was Ben in love with Joyce? Was Joyce in love with Ben? Why were they hiding their relationship from me? Would I have minded if they had told me? Too bloody right, I would have minded! I had always thought that Ben and I were actually made for each other, even though I knew I was going to leave and start my life path journey all over again.

If I had not had the persistent heartache caused by my love for Professor Malcolm James McKenzie, I would have been honoured to be Ben's wife and lifelong partner. So it was what it was, and I deserved this hurt. I had no right to come between Joyce and Ben. *Good luck to them*, I thought.

A couple of hours into my journey, my mobile started to ring. Of course, it was Joyce and then Ben, and then Joyce followed by Ben. I did not answer my phone at all. I did not want to speak to them ever again. What was done was done.

I phoned Cousin Emma and told her to expect Brutus and me the following day. Once in France, Brutus and I stayed at a small motel en route, and before long we arrived at Emma and Jeff's French cottage.

Emma and Jeff were so pleased to see Brutus and me. Indeed, I was so pleased and happy to be there with Emma and Jeff—the only people in the whole world that I loved and could be loved by in return without any judgement or expectation.

Over the following few weeks, I made many decisions—especially with regard to my future. I decided to make a home for myself and Brutus in France, preferably within easy distance to Emma and Jeff.

I enjoyed every new day, and I enjoyed the search for a property to make a home out of Joyce and Ben gave up trying to contact me, and I turned my phone off permanently when I purchased myself a brand-new, state-of-the-art, French phone.

Every day was a joy! I met new friends, and I visited many new places. My social life was fun and relaxing. Even Brutus seemed content and happier than he was before. Brutus and I still did everything together. Where I went, so did he.

The money I received from the insurance payout for the burnt-out cottage was more than enough to see me in a good position to find and purchase a small dwelling that would leave me plenty of money left over for living expenses, until I decided whether or not to find employment.

I had been in France for about three months when I received a call on my mobile from a new friend, Joe Sallik, who excitedly told me he had found a delightful small house for sale, and he was most insistent I should meet him and go and view said house.

I wasted no time at all, and after putting Brutus in the car, I drove to the meeting place that Joe had arranged for me. Joe joined me in my car, and within minutes we had arrived at the house that was for sale.

I fell in love with that beautiful old French house the first moment I saw it! It was so much like the cottage I had lost to the fire.

I walked around the outside of the house (which was empty), and I walked through the large overgrown garden to the rear. I tried looking through the windows, but I could not see the inside. I was so excited.

"Joe, this is wonderful. Please help me contact the agents with a view to them coming here as soon as possible so I can look inside. Oh, Joe, I am so thrilled. Please hurry and phone them. I must not lose this house!"

"I will do my best, but I don't think they will come out straight away," said Joe as he dialled the telephone number.

"Well, it must be your lucky day, Pauline. A woman called Mrs. Reeds, an English woman, is on her way. She will be with us within the hour," said Joe.

"Wonderful. Now the fun begins!" I replied, and we both laughed.

Joe Sallik was a middle-aged French man who lived on his own next door to Emma and Jeff. He was a ladies' man who was very good looking and had a lovable personality. I had heard that he had been married three times—need I say more? Like most Frenchmen, he was always smartly dressed. He was a little overweight but not fat, of medium height, and had dark brown longish hair and brown eyes. He lived next door to Emma and Jeff in a small holding he used for hen keeping. He produced a considerable amount of hen eggs for the local shops and markets, and he employed two or three French women for this business. From the look of him, I presumed that he was quite a wealthy man.

As I waited impatiently for Mrs. Reeds, I ran through the overgrown rear garden with Brutus. Brutus seemed happy with the place, and I was just keeping my fingers crossed that the inside of the house was as good as the outside.

The outside of the house was so similar to that of my previous cottage. There was a door in the centre of the front, with a window on either side of it. Three windows were on the first floor. The house was built of red brick with white windows and doors. It was so pretty and small. There was no front garden; the house just sat at the side of the footpath on a small country road.

At last, Mrs. Reeds arrived. After we were introduced, she opened the front door, and I raced in to view each room as quickly as I could. It was perfect. Each room was old and neglected. It needed plenty of tender, loving care, and I was the person who could give it that!

The ground floor, as with my previous cottage, had one large lounge and, at the back, one small kitchen. Upstairs there were two bedrooms and a bathroom and toilet. The lounge even had a wood burner in it. It was truly fantastic!

Whilst I was upstairs, Joe came to join me.

"Well, from the look on your face, I presume this is a house you would love to have!" he remarked.

"Most definitely. I don't even know what the price of it is. Do I make an offer? Is it up for auction? Please, Joe, go and get me some information," I said.

As Joe disappeared downstairs, I looked out of all the windows. Each window had a beautiful view of the countryside and part of the village nearby. Mrs. Reeds then got in her car and drove away.

"Joe, Joe!" I shouted. "Mrs. Reeds has gone. What has happened?"

"Calm down, Pauline!" said Joe as he laughed. "Mrs. Reeds has returned to her office. When you have finished viewing this property, she wishes you to return the keys to her. It is pretty obvious that you are more than interested in this house!"

"I am going to buy this house and make it into my home! What do I do next? Do I make an offer? I don't even know what the asking price is. Do you?" I asked.

Joe and I sat in the small kitchen, and Joe told me about the asking price. It was considerably less than I imagined it to be. Joe advised me to get a structural report and then make an offer if I wanted to proceed.

Well, I was not concerned about obtaining reports; I wanted that small French house, and I went with my instincts. Later that day I returned the keys to Mrs. Reed and made an offer for her to communicate to the seller.

My offer was accepted, and within days my solicitor and the seller's solicitor had exchanged contracts, and all monies were paid over. All done!

It is common practise in France for the agents to meet the new owners at the property in question after all monies have been paid, to give them the deed and the keys. When I met up with Mrs. Reeds to collect my documents and keys, it came to my attention that the field to the side of the house had also been sold to me and was noted on the deeds.

When Mrs. Reeds had left, Brutus and I just stood there in our new home. What a wonderful feeling that was!

Over the following months, Brutus and I moved into our new home. Joe had arranged for a local builder to inspect the property, and he found nothing to be concerned about. Only cosmetic work was required. I did not even want a new bathroom or new kitchen. I decorated all the rooms, and Joe cut my long, overgrown back garden. I agreed to allow Joe to use the field for his business as long as he made me a small parking place on hard standing material at the side of the house.

I was in desperate need of new furniture for nearly every room: beds, chairs, sofas, a small dining suite, wardrobes, and carpets and rugs. But in the short term, I entertained friends and family as it was. It was beautiful!

While Joe was busy on his mowing machine, clearing and cutting all the long grass and weeds, I began to notice that Joe was always around, helping and being ever so attentive. One day when he came into the kitchen for a drink, I decided it would be prudent of me to have "the talk."

I politely told Joe that I appreciated all his help and advice and that I was so thankful we were the best of friends. I also added that I was glad we were not romantically involved, as that would spoil our very special relationship. Joe did not comment, and from the way he looked at me, I knew it would be sensible of me to expect some problems from Joe.

Once my rear garden had been cleared, there was no need of Joe to come around and help me anymore. I was far too busy decorating all the rooms to give Joe a second thought.

Every day was a joy. I would busy myself by going to the decorator's store, and then I would clean up, strip the walls, hang wallpaper, and paint. The house became alive and ever so cosy. Brutus loved his rear garden and of course my bed and his place in front of the fire in the lounge.

I had many visitors. I made new friends and acquaintances. The time came when I was ready to have an official housewarming party.

Emma and Jeff loved to visit Brutus and me, and they would take us out for meals and to meet more new friends.

I invited as many people as I could to my house-warming party. Emma and Jeff also invited people—probably the whole of the local village.

The weather was brilliant on the night of my party. Jeff brought his barbecue, and Emma and I made sandwiches, cakes, sweets, and even homemade wine. Once everything had been prepared, Emma and Jeff went home to get changed ready for the party. I spent a couple of hours resting and getting all dressed up. I wore a beautiful dress and high-heeled shoes, not forgetting to put on make-up and do my hair properly.

I don't think any of my guests had previously seen me all dressed up and looking like a beautiful woman.

As I greeted my guests, I received plenty of compliments—especially from the men folk. When Joe arrived, the surprise on his face when he saw me standing there was a picture. Joe greeted me with a kiss on the lips, and then he commented on how beautiful and sexy I looked. I loved all the compliments, and I was pleased that all the dirty decorating jobs had finally finished and I could be myself and look good all the time. I told myself I had a new lease on life.

Everybody seemed to enjoy the night. There was plenty drink and food, and loud music from speakers outside led to dancing and merriment.

I danced with Joe many times, and I loved the feel of him holding me as a slow record played. I should have known better, but the party was in full flow and everyone was drinking, including Joe and me.

The last of my guests left in the early hours of the following morning. I knew Joe was still hanging around, so I told him I could manage to clean up and that he should go home. He would have none of that suggestion.

It was inevitable that Joe was the last guest left.

"Sorry, Joe, I am going to have to ask you to leave, as I am very tired now. I will clean up in the morning."

Joe did not answer. I looked into his eyes, and I knew he was going to try something on.

"Come on, Joe! I am not interested in whatever you are thinking about. Do you understand what I am trying to say?"

"All right, Pauline! Just let me kiss you, and I will leave. You have my word!"

I was quite drunk, and I stupidly agreed to his terms. I walked over to him, and he put his arms around me and placed his lips on mine. Ever so gently, we kissed. It was pleasant, and I reacted to his physical touch. That kiss became a very sexual kiss. Joe's hands were on my breasts, squeezing them hard. At the same time, he was manoeuvring me towards the stairs. We both fell onto the bottom stairs, and all I could feel was one of the wooden stairs hurting my back. At the same time, I could feel the weight of Joe on top of me. I could not move out of that position, and Joe had managed to put his hands up my skirt and was doing his best to remove my underwear. At the same time, he undid his trousers.

The feel of his body weighing me down and his smell brought back all the bad memories I had of my husband Gerald. I recalled, so vividly, Gerald walking across the landing and into my bedroom, where he always insisted that I remove my clothing and lie there while he used and abused me.

I screamed at Joe to stop what he was trying to do and let me get up off the stairs. Brutus had realised that someone was trying to hurt me, so he joined in, barking and snarling. Joe reluctantly got up off me and adjusted his clothing. He helped me to get up from the stairs.

"I am so sorry, Pauline. I did not mean for it to happen like that! You have been teasing me for weeks, so I presumed you would want to have sex with me."

"You are a dear, dear friend. If I had any romantic ideas toward you, I would want our first sex to be something special, not a quickie on the stairs. I know you realise that now, so please, Joe, go home and we can both forget this sorry incident."

Not another word was spoken. Joe left the house, and I locked the door behind him. I retired to bed and hugged Brutus all night.

The next morning, I was woken by banging at my front door and, of course, Brutus barking at the visitor outside.

I quickly dressed and went downstairs and opened the door. I was relieved to see Emma there and not Joe. Emma rushed in past me. She was all excited and was waving a piece of paper.

"Guess! Guess! Guess what I am holding in my hand!" shouted Emma, all excited.

"Have you won the Euro Millions lottery?" I said sarcastically. "Better than that!" replied Emma.

"For goodness' sake, Emma, I have a very bad hangover, and I do not feel like playing your game!" I said, grinding my teeth.

"Sit down, and I will make you a coffee. Jeff has received an invitation to a hotel in London to attend the Lifetime Achievement Awards Ceremony. Guess who has won the Lifetime Achievement Award for Services to the Police Force?" said an excited and proud Emma.

"I have no idea, but I am sure you are going to tell me," I again sarcastically remarked.

"Jeff! Jeff! He is over the moon that he is going to be recognised for all his police work over all those years!

We shall get a party of friends and us, and we shall go to London and maybe stay for a week to incorporate the award ceremony and a short holiday. What do you think?" asked Emma.

"Sorry, Emma. Yes, it is wonderful, and I myself shall look forward to a break away. I feel very proud to know Jeff. You must feel very proud of Jeff. I am so hungover this morning that I don't think my brain is working. It is a couple of weeks away from Christmas; when is the ceremony?" I asked.

"The first week of February. Full evening dress for both men and women is the dress code. I shall probably have to spend some time online to purchase both myself and Jeff suitable attire."

I managed to survive Emma's excited morning outburst. I was relieved when she left, and after a couple of cups of coffee, I started to feel better. With only a couple of weeks to go before Christmas, I wanted to buy a Christmas tree and decorate it. My first Christmas in my new French home was going to be so special.

Christmas arrived, and as happens with all good Christmases, so did the snow. Christmas Day was to be celebrated at Emma and Jeff's, and I was to entertain family and friends on Boxing Day. Joe was still my closest friend. He never mentioned the night of my house-warming, and neither did I. It was as if it had never happened, although I could still tell he was somewhat infatuated with me. Joe had many female friends, so I did not give him a second thought. A French woman once told me of a saying which describes perfectly my feelings towards Joe: "He does not light my fire."

Once Christmas was well and truly over, it was time for us all to plan for Jeff's award ceremony.

I, Jeff, Emma, Joe, and a few friends of Emma and Jeff's were to travel to the hotel that was hosting the awards, and we were to stay there for a week. That would give us all plenty of time to really treat the outing as a holiday.

I did not require a new outfit for the special night, as I had a beautiful evening dress I had bought in a charity shop. It was perfect. It was knitted silk, green in colour, and it fit me perfectly. All I had to do was shop around for shoes, an evening bag, and jewellery. Within a few days, I had bought everything I needed, and I treated myself to some outdoor day clothes for wearing on sightseeing trips.

I had always relied on Joe to look after Brutus if I was ever away for whatever reason. Joe had two black Labradors who played well with Brutus. They were both bitches, and Joe had expressed a desire to use Brutus to breed with them. Brutus had never been around when his dogs were in season, but there would be a very good chance that this might occur while we were away in London. As Joe was to be in our party, he arranged for his brother to take all three dogs whilst we were away. I had no objection to that at all.

CHAPTER 9

Reunited

A FTER WEEKS OF PLANNING and preparation, we all arrived at the hotel in London. We had all travelled together in a large minibus. Jeff was the driver, and we all relaxed and enjoyed the journey there. The large hotel was situated on the outskirts of Hyde Park. We were all excited as we were taken to our respective rooms. My room had the most fantastic view of Hyde Park, and it seemed that everyone in our party had similar rooms. Brilliant! I thought.

We spent the day of our arrival just relaxing after the journey. The following day was the day that the awards ceremony was to be held at night, so that day was a day for getting ready for the evening dinner dance and the actual awards.

That evening, we all met up at the bar. We had drinks all around before we were shown to our table for the evening dinner, prior to the entertainment and awards. One large round table seated our party. The men in our party looked handsome and magnificent in their dinner suits, and the ladies in our party looked beautiful and magnificent in their evening dresses. I thought I looked very good—especially as it had been some time since I had had cause to dress up.

We all took our seats. On each place setting was a highly glossed brochure that had been produced to celebrate the occasion.

As the wine flowed and we were all making ourselves comfortable, I quickly perused the fancy brochure. On one page, it listed all the recipients for each of the awards. I was busy trying to see if I could find Jeff Lloyd's name when I came across something that sent me into shock.

This is what I read: "Professor Malcolm James McKenzie for the Lifetime Achievement Award for Services to the Nuclear Scientific Industry".

It took me a little time to compose myself. *Will Malcolm be here in person? Will he be represented by someone else? If he is to be here, will I meet him? If he is to be represented, will I be able to get a contact address or phone number for him?* All these thoughts were rushing around in my head.

I was seated facing away from the band and the stage. I desperately wanted to turn around and look at all the other tables to see if I could find him. I knew it would look ridiculous if I were to turn and stir at people, so I sat there and wondered how I was to act if I met him and talked to him.

As I sat looking forward towards the bar area, I saw him! There he was—Professor Malcolm James McKenzie! He was with a party of both men and women. I recognised his sister, but I could not make out if Malcolm was with any particular woman. Malcolm looked so distinguished and smart. He had not changed at all.

My heart started to beat fast in my chest. Nervousness came over me.

I had loved Malcolm since the first time we had met. I really thought he was attracted to me like I was to him. We had kissed sexually on more than one occasion—the last being the day he disappeared out of my life.

My heart was pounding. I could feel that my face was hot and flushed. I could not make out what the people on my table were talking about. I was fixed on watching Malcolm.

Malcolm and his party were shown to their table, which was behind where I was seated and way off to the left of the room. I lost sight of where his table was.

The wine was still flowing, and everyone in my party was laughing and talking. I knew I had to compose myself and enjoy the evening and the awards for Jeff's sake, if not for anyone else.

The dinner was superb. We all enjoyed the food and the drink. Towards the end of the dinner, the band started to play. They were loud and wonderful.

When all dishes had been cleared from all the tables, coffee, biscuits, and liquors were served, and everyone in that ballroom prepared for the compére to start the important proceedings.

By this time, I had decided to play it cool with Malcolm if I were to meet him at al. He had not bothered to contact me. He just disappeared with his sister. It had been over four years since I had seen him, and I had loved him all that time.

The lifetime achievement awards were given to maybe fifty or so recipients who worked in various occupations, various charities, various sports, and the like.

I had the brochure in front of me at all times as I waited to see Malcolm, when it was his special time. Malcolm, like Jeff, when called, had to go onto the stage area to receive his award from a member of the royal family.

Jeff received his award before Malcolm. The whole room applauded Jeff, and our small party celebrated in a noisy style. It was very exciting to be part of the whole celebration.

The time arrived for Malcolm to be presented with his award. Many people were standing to applaud him, so I stood to get a better view of him.

He looked just as I remembered him: tall, well-groomed, balding on top of his head, and good-looking in his own right. He was such a confident, accomplished man.

My heart was beating so fast. I could feel an excited sexual thrill running all through my body. I was still in love with him! I knew I had suffered unrequited love for Malcolm since I first met him all that time ago.

The awards drew to a close. Within minutes, the large room partition was folded away, revealing a fantastic dance floor. The band started up, and as the music flowed loudly across the whole area, people flocked to dance.

There Malcolm was, dancing with a gorgeous woman! They laughed and talked, and they danced well together. Was I to presume that they might be an item? I sat there quietly, realising that I should not seek him out. He had disappeared from the area where I lived without so much as a goodbye. He probably never had any romantic ideas towards me. I could have been living under a misconception that there were some feelings of love between us. I felt it was best I leave things alone!

I enjoyed the rest of the night with the beautiful people in our party. It was a great success, and the compére closed the ceremony. We all applauded the band, and the large room and dance floor emptied quickly.

Joe and Jeff decided they would like a coffee and a few more drinks before they retired. I agreed to go with them, and after saying goodnight to the rest of the party, we made our way into the hotel and headed straight for the hotel bar.

I sat at a small table in the bar, and as I looked up, I found I was looking straight at Malcolm, who was seated directly opposite to me. As I looked at him, he was looking back at me. Our eyes met, and I had all those sensuous feelings running all over me. I smiled, and Malcolm returned with a smile and a wink.

I turned away and made polite conversation with Joe and Jeff.

Within minutes, Malcolm was standing beside me. He quickly placed a chair at the side of me and sat down.

"Sorry to interrupt, but I just had to come and see how you were. I am so pleased to see you after all this time. You look wonderful, Pauline!"

"Well thank you, kind sir," I said, and we both laughed. "May I introduce my award-winning brother-in-law, Jeff, and my friend Joe.

We all made light conversation, and Jeff and Joe said their goodnights and left.

Malcolm ordered more coffees and brandies. We talked and laughed about what had happened to each of us, over the past years. I knew I had to be strong and not read anything into his attitude towards me.

Malcolm told me that he and his sister had moved into a very large house in Southern England. He worked in America with a group of other nuclear scientists, and his sister Amy lived in England and ran the house. Malcolm said he needed a large house for it to be a base for him and somewhere he could entertain friends and colleagues.

"So you and Ben Wilcock did not get married?" asked Malcolm. I shook my head and laughed. He continued, "I really thought you and Ben would have married. He was very fond of you."

Pity I could not tell him that it was because of him, and the fact that I was in love with him, that I never married Ben Wilcock. "Have you married, Malcolm, or are you in a relationship?"

"Good grief, no! I am a free spirit, and it does not help that my work takes me all over the world. I never know where I will be or for how long I will be there. In a few months, I am to retire. My life will be my own for me to choose what I do, and where, and for how long!" We both laughed. "I am leaving tomorrow. We must not lose touch with one another this time. At breakfast, I will give you my card, and perhaps you can give me your contact number."

I nodded in agreement, and I was secretly pleased and excited.

"Well Malcolm, it was lovely meeting you again, but I must retire now. It has been a very long day!" I said, and as I started to leave the bar, Malcolm shook my hand.

What a weird person he is—very self-centred, I thought as I made my way to my room.

I could not sleep properly that night. I was excited at the prospect that I might, at long last, be able to see more of Malcolm. I could hardly wait for breakfast time to come. I made myself look good, and I looked forward to seeing Malcolm even though he was leaving that morning.

I joined Emma and Jeff at their breakfast table. I looked around the restaurant, but there was no sign of Malcolm or his sister. He never did show for breakfast. Malcolm and his party must have already left. I was gutted! The promise of exchanging contact numbers was no more! He had disappeared again, without even a goodbye, just as he had done years before.

That day, our small party of relatives and friends hopped on and off the London tour buses. We saw as many London sites as we could. Exhausted and hungry, we returned to our hotel. When I was given my room key by the reception attendant, there was an envelope with it. I did not open the envelope until I was alone in my room. I thought it was a bill from the hotel or something similar, so it was a great shock to find that it was a note from Malcolm.

As promised, enclosed is my business card.

Sorry I cannot see you this morning. A change of plan meant that we were all to leave early. Please text me to let me know you have received this note. I hope you won't mind that once I have your phone number, I would like to contact you.

Lovely to meet you again.

Kind regards, Malcolm.

I danced around my bedroom, holding his card. I was excited and relieved that we had not lost touch this time, and I immediately texted confirmation of my receipt of his card and said that I hoped his return journey was good.

For the remaining days of our holiday, I was constantly watching my phone, waiting for Malcolm to contact me. He never did! When I returned home to France, I was still watching my phone, waiting for Malcolm to contact me. He never did! I did not want to phone or text Malcolm. I had to be sure he was the one to make the first move.

Brutus was so pleased to see me, and of course I was so pleased to see Brutus. I was happy to return to my lovely house. A few weeks went by, and one day I finally received a phone call from Malcolm. I knew that in a way I was expecting a call from him, but it was still a shock when he did finally call.

Malcolm sounded very relaxed, and he made no mention of the length of time that had passed before he phoned me. He invited me to his home for Easter. It was his sister's birthday, and she had arranged a large party.

"Amy is the hostess, and I am the host, but what I would really enjoy is you, Pauline, being my plus one."

I gratefully accepted, and Malcolm said he had worked out and planned my journey. I gave him my email address, and he forwarded me all the details of my travel plans.

Once I had received Malcolm's email, I was on cloud nine. At last I had something to look forward to—the ability to move on from pining for someone who had shown no interest in me.

Easter was soon to be with us. In Malcom's travel instructions, he had mentioned a small airport near his house. He mentioned the airport nearest to where I lived that serviced that airport. The day and the details of the flight and times were all quoted, and he instructed me to get a taxi to his house, the address of which he had noted for me.

I could only presume that I had told Malcolm whereabouts in France I lived when we were chatting that night in the hotel. I could not remember mentioning my home in France, but I had had plenty to drink that night.

I booked a return flight and prepared myself for a visit to Malcolm's home. I made sure that when I packed my case for a week's visit to Malcolm's that I had made allowances for clothes for every occasion. I so wanted to make a strong and lasting impression.

When the day came, I was so excited. Brutus had gone to stay with Joe, and Emma took me to the airport. When I landed after just a one-hour flight, I followed Malcolm's instructions and took a taxi to Malcolm's house.

The taxi drove down a short drive to the front door. As we arrived, Amy came out to greet me. The house was a huge Georgian house which was surrounded by landscaped gardens. It was truly beautiful!

"Lovely to see you again, Pauline; I hope your journey went well," said Amy.

"All according to plan. No problems at all," I replied.

"Come; I will make some refreshments, and then I will give you a guided tour and show you to your room. Malcolm has been delayed, as usual, but he will be here by the time we will have dinner."

Amy was so pleasant, and she told me she was looking forward to her birthday celebrations, which were to take place the following day along with a party for close friends and relatives in the evening. She told me that everything was ready and that caterers and music entertainers had all been arranged for the evening.

As promised, Amy gave me a tour of the house. I was most impressed by Malcolm's music room. The white grand piano was situated in the centre of the all-white room, with paintings on all walls. I recalled being seated at the very same piano when I visited Malcolm in the house he had lived in previously—the house situated opposite my small country cottage. I also recalled how, that night, I was impressed by Malcolm's talent as a musician and by his intelligence. I was besotted with Malcolm, and I yearned for Malcolm to hold me, kiss me, and perhaps fall in love with me as I had done with him. Well, that hadn't happened. Malcolm and his sister had just moved away!

The house was huge, and as I walked around the large room that was to be used as a dance floor area, I listened to Amy as she talked about Malcolm. She told me that his work was everything to him. He was a celebrated scientist and had had many achievements. Malcolm had never been married; he had many close women friends, but he had never wanted to settle down with any of them. Amy, on the other hand, had settled down with a woman she had known for years, and they were very happy together. Although Amy still lived with Malcolm, she had plans to move away with her partner when they had found suitable accommodation.

I wondered what would happen to Malcolm, after Amy had left to live her own life. He would definitely rattle in that huge house.

The ground floor accommodated five large double bedrooms, each with its own bathroom. Amy took me to one of the bedrooms and left me there while I unpacked and freshened up.

I changed into suitable clothing for meeting Malcolm and enjoying an evening meal with him and, of course, Amy. When ready, I made my way downstairs and into the kitchen, where Amy was giving the housekeeper her last-minute instructions.

"Well, Pauline, will you be all right in that bedroom?" asked Amy. "Yes. It is beautiful," I replied.

"We shall go into the lounge and wait for Malcolm, and when he arrives, we will be able to sit down and eat at last!"

With a glass of wine in hand, I chatted to Amy. We seemed to get on quite well. I was still feeling a little apprehensive about seeing Malcolm again.

It was not long before I heard a car arrive. Within minutes, Malcolm walked into the lounge, making his apologies for not being there when I arrived and for being later than he had expected.

I watched him as he poured himself a drink and talked with Amy. He was tall and good-looking, even though he was balding. He was a very distinguished gentleman. My heart was pounding, and I was feeling a little nervous. I so wanted to make an impression on Malcolm.

It was a lovely dinner, and the three of us relaxed and chatted. When the housekeeper had cleared the table after the meal and left for the night, so did Amy. She just disappeared. I presumed that she had gone out to meet her lady friend.

Malcolm invited me to join him in the lounge, and as we sat by the blazing fire, drinking wine, we talked and laughed together. He made no mention of Brutus, which surprised me, as he knew how much Brutus meant to me. To be honest, his main conversation was all about himself. It was great to be seated with him and every now and again our eyes met, and I felt the sexual energy all over my body. There was no contact between us—not even hand-holding.

Towards the end of the night, Malcolm said that he would have to excuse himself, as he was extremely tired. He had been travelling all day, and all he wanted to do was shower and sleep. I agreed that I also was becoming tired, so I said goodnight and made my way to my room.

Malcolm made no effort to politely kiss me goodnight, so I just sat on my bed and wondered whether he was pleased to see me or not.

The next day, the day of Amy's birthday bash, I woke to the sounds of the countryside. Malcolm had suggested that we enjoy the surrounding countryside today, so, dressed accordingly, I made my way downstairs into the kitchen dining area.

I sat with Amy and Malcolm, and the housekeeper served a cooked breakfast to us all. Amy was very argumentative with Malcolm, and as I felt uneasy about it, I remained quiet and ate my breakfast.

When Amy stormed out of the room, Malcolm just sat there in silence and ate his breakfast. Eventually Malcolm turned to me and said, "Sorry, Pauline; Amy can be so awkward at times." "I was wondering if you realised that I was sat at the same table as you! A word from you and I might have felt a little better!" I hissed those words out, as I was so angry; I thought Malcolm should have been more bothered about his guest than his sister.

"You are right," replied Malcolm. "Sorry! Listen, I will make it up to you. We shall have a good walk around this area, and I will treat you to the best pub lunch you have ever had."

That day, we walked slowly for miles. Sometimes we held hands, and sometimes we linked arms. We talked, we relaxed, we laughed, and once, whilst trying to climb over a wall, we kissed. We kissed as lovers did. I loved the feeling of Malcolm kissing me, and I knew he enjoyed every minute of that kiss.

After a fantastic pub lunch, we made our way back to the house to prepare for the evening festivities. I was relieved to be in the privacy of my room. I needed a rest before I prepared myself for the party.

I must have fallen asleep on the bed. When I woke, I realised that I had very little time to get ready properly.

I rushed around like a madwoman, and eventually I was ready to go downstairs and join the party.

As I entered the large party room, I noticed Malcolm talking to a beautiful woman. He had his arm around her waist, and he was laughing with her. I stood there for a little while, waiting for my host to come over and welcome me to the party. It was a little time before Malcolm came over to greet me.

"What time do you call this?" whispered Malcolm. I was angry and disappointed with Malcolm. "What time do you want to call it, Malcolm?" I angrily whispered back.

Malcolm looked furious. "Do you want me to go and get you a drink?" asked Malcolm.

"Not if you don't want to; I can always get my own!" I retaliated, and with that I walked away and headed for the wine table. Malcolm did not follow me; the beautiful woman joined him, and they continued their conversation.

I was far too angry to be upset. A very polite man came to my rescue and asked me to dance. I politely refused, so he found somewhere for us to sit and chat. He introduced himself as Allan, Malcolm's neighbour. After quite a while, Malcolm joined us.

"Do you want to dance?" asked Malcolm. "No thank you. Do you?" I replied.

"No, not really. I don't dance very well. I usually avoid all dancing," Malcolm replied.

When Allan had left us, we sat in silence.

"I am not doing very well—with you, I mean. Sorry, Pauline; I am making a complete mess of this. I was angry that you had made me wait for you tonight. I am not used to being kept waiting."

"So you decided to be off with me because of that?" I asked.

"Listen, can we please start again?" replied Malcolm. "I am fed up of bickering. I have enough of that from Amy."

The rest of the evening was a complete success. Amy had a wonderful time. So did I, and so did Malcolm.

Malcolm and I danced until the early hours of the morning. When everyone had gone home, Malcolm walked me upstairs to my room and politely said goodnight. He then retired to his room. He did not even give me a goodnight kiss! There was no passion from him. He had no intention of seducing me, even though he must have been aware that I really wanted some love and affection from him.

The rest of my week staying at Malcolm's home went pretty much the same as the first day. Amy never seemed to be at home. The housekeeper ran the house and always provided us with a delicious dinner. Malcolm and I would go out for the day. We visited some beautiful places, and on two occasions we went to the cinema. Even visiting a large garden centre with Malcolm was interesting.

Each day, there was some private time for Malcolm and me. Sometimes we would kiss and cuddle, and other times we would walk holding each other very closely; but there was never a time when Malcolm showed any desire for me, and he definitely showed no passion for me.

I found having a conversation with him was hard. He seemed to be interested only in his work and the places he had visited over the years. He never spoke of his private life, so I had no idea if he had ever been in love. I knew he had never married, but that was all I knew. I found Malcolm to be a very boring, selfish person. He was not the person I thought I had fallen in love with.

I was looking forward to going home to my small house, to Brutus and to Joe, and to Emma, Jeff, and all my other friends.

At last I was on the flight home. Emma collected me from the airport, and we chatted excitedly all the way back to my small house. I never voiced concerns about my feelings for Malcolm to Emma. I think the reason I never talked to Emma about them was that deep down I knew she would tell me what I already knew—that it was obvious Malcolm was not the man for me.

Malcolm told me he would phone me after I had arrived home. I knew he would not, but this time I did not watch my phone for a call from him. I knew he would contact me at some point, but I was not in a hurry to see him again soon.

That night, curled up in front of my fire with Brutus by my side, I went on the Internet, to check my emails.

There was an email from my solicitor. He wrote that a Mr.Ben Wilcock from Wilcock Farm had an interest in purchasing, from me, the land that my burnt- out cottage stood on. He said that it was overgrown and that it would complement his grazing pasture to the rear and provide a good access point for his farm vehicles as well as livestock. Ben Wilcock had stated that if I were interested in selling said plot of land, he would obtain an independent valuation and would proceed with an offer.

I was aware that the plot my old cottage stood on was not really worth anything, but curiosity got the better of me. I decided to look up all planning applications for the area around my old cottage, just in case there was some sinister plot that Ben Wilcock was part of.

With a large brandy in my hand, I viewed the local paper for the area I used to live in. In each weekly edition, planning applications were noted. I looked at all previous copies of the weekly journal on the Internet, some of which went back as far as eighteen months previous.

I had only just started my search when I was surprised to find, in the Announcements section, that a Mr. Ben Wilcock and Miss Joyce Macey were announcing their engagement. There was a small, pleasant photo of the happy couple and a note saying that they were to marry soon.

I was shocked and bewildered. Joyce sleeping with and having sex with Ben was one thing, but I never thought of them as wanting to be married. How wrong could I have been!

I had to be honest with myself. Yes, I was hurt. Ben was not mine. He could have been, but I had not wanted that. I tried to think kindly about their engagement, but it was too hard a pill to swallow.

I was quite shaken, so I decided against looking at all the local planning applications. If Ben had intentions to cheat me, then I would let him! I did not care. That announcement was dated some eighteen months earlier, so it stood to reason that Ben and Joyce would have been married over a year ago.

I replied to my solicitor that I had no objection to Mr. Ben Wilcock making me an offer for said plot of land.

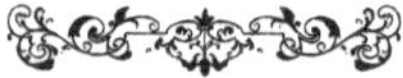

During the next few weeks at home, I busied myself with completing all the decorating and started on landscaping my large rear garden. I tried not to think about or dwell on Ben and Joyce. I tried to wish them all the happiness their marriage would bring, but I was still feeling somewhat cheated!

At last, a few weeks after I had left Malcolm's, I received a phone call from him. He wanted me to join him at his home for a couple of weeks while he was not working.

"Sorry; I have been so busy I could not phone to arrange anything with you, but now I have a couple of weeks free. It would be great for us to be together again.

Amy has moved out, so apart from my house keeper, we shall have the place to ourselves. What do you think? I was thinking of going to the south coast for a couple of days in a pleasant small hotel I know. Do you fancy that as well?" asked an excited Malcolm.

"Yes, that sounds good," I replied. "I feel as if I am in need of a distraction. Do your usual and email me my flight details, and I will contact you as soon as I have booked everything. And also I need to check with Joe that he can look after Brutus for me."

As per my instructions, I arranged for Joe to have Brutus, and I booked my return flight.

It was true that Amy had moved out. She had gone to live with her female partner.

It was a pleasant two weeks, and we spent a few days staying in a small hotel on the south coast.

When I realised that Malcolm had booked two separate rooms in the hotel, I was not pleased or flattered. I needed to know where I stood with him.

One night, before we set off for the hotel on the coast, I cuddled up to him on the sofa in front of a large open fire. Malcolm was playing some CDs whilst reading some of his work papers.

"Malcolm, can I talk to you for a moment?" I whispered shyly. "Hmm, yes, what?" asked Malcolm.

"I have always loved you since we first met. I know you do not love me yet, but I need to know if you find me attractive, and I need to know if you ever feel that you want to make love to me? I mean, do you want to have sex with me?" I was so embarrassed saying that to Malcolm.

Malcolm seemed shocked at my boldness. "Pauline, let me put it this way. I will have no problem having sex with you. You are a beautiful, sexy woman. My problem is that we do not know each other well enough to start an intimate relationship—not yet anyway. Do you not agree?"

"I don't know," I whispered. "I wanted us to have a loving relationship with plenty of affection, and I presumed that we would enjoy that as well as making love to each other. It is all part of the same relationship I wanted with you."

"I also want a loving relationship with you, Pauline, but that does not mean that we have to be intimate yet. There will be plenty of time for sex when our relationship moves on to another level.Please say that you understand."

"I suppose I do, but life is too short to start planning things out. Anyway, forget I ever said anything, and let us just enjoy what will do us both good," I replied, trying to sound positive.

"That's my girl! We have plenty of good times ahead of us, and I do love you; never doubt that!"

Over the following few months and well into autumn, I travelled back and forth to and from Malcolm's. Joe was good enough to look after Brutus, and although I invited Malcolm to come and stay with me and meet my cousin Emma and Jeff, Malcolm refused every invitation. He said that he was far too busy while he was working. He said that once he retired, which would be soon, he would have more time to socialise with me in France.

On each and every occasion on which I went to stay with Malcolm, I could feel my love for him waver. I was feeling bored with his attitude and his constant conversation about himself. He was a selfish man. I no longer desired him to touch me sexually. In fact, I did not fancy him sexually as much as I used to. I was relieved and much happier, when I was at home in my French house with my beloved dog, Brutus.

It was late autumn when Malcolm phoned and said he was to retire. He and Amy were going to arrange a good retirement party at Malcolm's house. As per usual, Malcolm said he would email me all my flight details, and he instructed me to bring an evening dress, as the theme for the party would be Bond 007, with all the men in evening suits and all the women in evening dresses.

I must admit that the thought of Malcolm not having any work to go to made me wonder if our relationship would last.

A few days before I was due to fly out to Malcolm's, I noticed that Brutus was not himself. Within hours, Brutus was lying on the floor vomiting, and he had started with severe diarrhoea.

I frantically phoned Joe, who immediately came to see Brutus.

As soon as he saw Brutus, I could see by the look on his face that this was serious.

"I will call the vet," said Joe. "He needs to come straight away to see Brutus."

Within an hour, the vet arrived and told me he was taking Brutus to the animal hospital. It all happened so quickly, and I was in bits! The vet said Brutus was very poorly with the parvovirus. It is usually fatal, but there was a chance that if the animal hospital could stop Brutus's dehydration, he might stand a chance.

I stood by Brutus' cage in the animal hospital. Brutus had drips going into each limb. They did not need to sedate Brutus, as he was so poorly; he just lay there. His eyes were closed, and he seemed to be struggling to breathe.

I phoned Malcolm and apologised for the fact that I would not be attending his retirement party. I told Malcolm, how poorly Brutus was and that there had been no change in his condition and that the vet had told me to expect the worst.

What happened next changed my feelings for Malcolm forever. I had to listen to Malcolm rant over the fact that I was not going to be at his retirement party because of a stupid dog.

"For goodness' sake, Pauline, it is only a dog! How dare you choose a bloody dog over me! Now you get on that plane as planned, and we will forget all the upset you have caused!" shouted Malcolm down the phone.

I never went to Malcolm's retirement party. I refused to speak to him. I stayed at Brutus's side for over three days. On the fourth day, there were signs of improvement, and by the sixth day, Brutus was recovering well.

That was one of the worst times in my life.

I was so relieved when Brutus was finally back home with me. I vowed never to leave him again. To hell with Malcolm, his sister, and all his crony friends. I owed Brutus's recovery to the fast actions of my good friend Joe. I would be in his debt forever!

For quite a few weeks, I refused to speak to Malcolm. I would not answer his calls. I did not want to know such a self-centred, selfish man. He did not love me. If he did love me, he would have understood my pain and anguish.

All Malcolm was interested in was Malcolm!

Winter was settling in. Malcolm and I had started talking again, and Malcolm was so sorry that he had upset me so much. He wanted me to spend Christmas with him, but I flatly refused. There was no way I wanted to be anywhere else but my home in France with Brutus, my friends, and my family. I told Malcolm that he was very welcome to stay with me in France over Christmas, but he refused because he needed to be with Amy and her partner. So be it, I thought.

Eventually Malcolm and I came to a compromise. The weekend before Christmas, I would drive to Malcolm's house and stay there for just a couple of days. I needed to drive, as I did not want to take a chance on flights being cancelled at that time of year for whatever reason. That would mean that Malcolm could stay at home for Christmas and be there for his sister Amy and her partner.

Malcolm said he had a surprise for me, and he wanted me to bring an evening dress with me.

As the weekend before Christmas arrived, I set off very early and drove all the way to Malcolm's home. I did not even stop for a night in a motel, which I usually did. I just wanted to get there and then get back home.

I was shocked when an excited Malcolm and Amy announced that they had arranged a Christmas Party for all their family and friends, to be held the day after I arrived.

"I have brought Christmas forward to accommodate you, Pauline," said Malcolm. "Amy and I are so looking forward to tomorrow night's Christmas party. I know you are exhausted, so a good meal tonight and a good night's rest, and tomorrow you will feel so much better."

"I am surprised you have done this for me; you really did not need to go to any trouble for me," I replied. I was really shocked, and I began to wish that I had never gone to Malcolm's house. All I wanted to do was go to Malcolm's for one last time. I knew our relationship was going nowhere, and I knew I no longer had any sort of feelings for Malcolm, physical or mental.

"I hope you brought an evening dress with you," said Malcolm. "Yes, I did as you requested," I said sarcastically.

I rested a little while in my room, and I unpacked the few clothes I had brought with me. After a lovely evening meal and a few drinks, I made my apologies to Malcolm and Amy as I explained that I needed to retire and rest up for the following day. I said goodnight and retired to my room. I was so relieved to have some privacy.

The day of the early Christmas party was quite a busy one. Malcolm had gone out early in the morning to get things for the evening meal, and I wandered around the house and the gardens, helping the housekeeper and Amy whenever I could.

It was early afternoon when Malcolm returned. He had purchased miniature perfumes for the lady guests, six in a box, and for the men, he had purchased boxes of miniature bottles of liqueurs.

As Malcolm placed these presents on the kitchen table, he asked if I would help Amy wrap them. Without any warning, Malcolm stood me up, put his arms around me, and kissed me in a very seductive way. Even Amy was surprised at his actions. I did not know what to think. I had no feelings left for him. Malcolm might have enjoyed that kiss, but it did not do anything for me and meant nothing to me.

The housekeeper was busy cooking turkey with all the trimmings and other meats for the table that evening. I finished wrapping the presents, and with a good large cup of tea in my hands, I headed back to the sanctuary of my room, where I was to stay until the evening festivities.

I took my time getting dressed and preparing myself for the early Christmas party.

I sat in front of the dressing table, and I was pleased with the way I looked. I wore the evening dress I had purchased from a charity shop many months before. It was a beautiful blue-and-green knitted silk dress, and I complemented it with some beautiful jewellery.

A knock on my door made me jump.

"Can I come in, Pauline?" asked Malcolm. "Of course!" I replied.

Malcolm stood behind me, and he looked at me through the mirror of the dressing table.

"You look gorgeous, Pauline!" he said, and again without any warning, he bent down and started to kiss my neck. As I tried to make my escape from his attentions, Malcolm shocked me again as he said, "You and I shall share the same bed tonight!"

"Is that a request, or is it an order?" I hissed those words at him.

"It is what we both want; that is what it is!" snapped Malcolm, and then we both made our way downstairs to greet all the guests.

With Malcolm and I seated at the top of the large dining table, the housekeeper and Amy prepared the drinks, gave out the presents, organised the music, and brought out all the Christmas fare that had been prepared and cooked.

The room looked fantastic, with a large decorated Christmas tree in the corner and a well-lit fire complementing the decorations.

The evening was very enjoyable, and as the coffee and liqueurs were being served, Malcolm held my left hand.

As quick as a flash, he placed a large diamond engagement ring on my finger. I had no time to react or think as Malcolm announced to everybody that I was going to be his wife.

There was cheering, shouting, kissing, and hugging. Mayhem broke out. I was very, very angry. He had not had the decency to ask me to marry him; he had, as usual, just presumed. And also as usual, he wanted all his own way.

There was no way I wanted to become Malcolm's wife. A few months previous, I probably would have been over the moon at the prospect of marrying him, but I had lost all love and respect for him.

There was nothing I could do apart from ruin everybody's night. So when all the guests had gone and Amy had left to join her partner, leaving Malcolm and I alone, I told him that he presumed too much, that I was not in love with him, that there was no way I would share his bed, and that as far as I was concerned we were well and truly over.

Conceited Malcolm just laughed and said it was obvious that I had had too much to drink. He thought it best that I go to my room (like a small child being punished) and that we discuss matters in the morning.

In the privacy of my guest bedroom, I sat and thought about what I should do for the best. I had had only two large glasses of wine, and I knew that in a little while I would be able to get in my car and drive away. I just wanted to get away from that place and Malcolm, and I desperately wanted to go home to France, where I was happy.

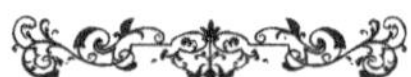

As I sat on the bed, feeling lost and so insecure, I glanced down at my hand. As I looked at the engagement ring, I thought to myself, *Gerald, my ex- husband, gave me a ring. It was a ring of control. Malcolm has just given me a ring—a ring of convenience. All I wanted was to one day be given*

a ring of love. I wanted to go in the direction of my dreams, and I wanted to live the life that I imagined. I wanted to dream without fear, and I wanted to love and be loved without limits.

I packed my case and dressed to travel. I waited until I knew Malcolm would be asleep. I placed the engagement ring on the dressing table. That would say it all to Malcolm.

Slowly and quietly, I made my way downstairs and into the kitchen. The back door was the only door that opened easily, and once I had opened it, I made my way to my car. Within minutes, I was driving away. I drove through the rest of the night and most of the following day, until I reached home.

Strangely, I never received any contact from Malcolm: no phone calls, no letters—no nothing. How could I have loved a man so much and then lost the love I had for him? How could I have loved a man for so long? How could I have put my life and happiness on hold for so long, waiting for a man—a man that I had not had time to get to know?

Over the next few days, after I had collected Brutus from Joe, I did not want to leave my house. I felt safe and secure with Brutus by my side. Apart from going for a daily walk and collecting some provisions, I used my time to put all my affairs in order.

I had so many emails, that I had not seen. Some were important—especially emails from my solicitor. It seemed that Ben Wilcock had had my plot of land valued by an independent valuer and accordingly made a generous offer for my plot. I replied to my solicitor and agreed to accept Ben's offer, and I asked him to prepare the necessary contract and land registry forms.

Christmas was wonderful with Emma and Jeff. I greatly appreciated all my friends and celebrations for the New Year; they gave me a new hope for the future. One thing I realised was that I could not keep running away from life's upsets and disappointments. I needed to start facing up to upsets and heartaches and not take the easy way out and leave without telling anyone. It was a coward's way out.

I thought about Joyce—my best friend and my business partner. I had just left her, leaving no forwarding address. I had left only a contact number for my solicitor. I had been too cowardly to face the truth, so I took the easy way out and left.

I thought about my lover Ben Wilcock. Again, I had been too cowardly to face the truth about him and Joyce, so I took the easy way out and left.

Even Malcolm deserved to have had one last conversation with me before I left for good, but no, I was too cowardly to face him, so I took the easy way out and left.

I knew that I had to change my attitude, as I was heading toward a lonely life. If I did not change my attitude, I would end up a lonely old woman.

A few weeks after New Year's Day, I received the contract for Ben Wilcock to purchase my plot of land. I was to sign it and post it to Ben Wilcock for the monies to be paid over. The land registry forms had all been completed, and there were copies of these that were to be posted with the signed contract.

I knew what I had to do. I was to take those legal papers personally to Ben Wilcock. It would give me the excuse to see Ben and Joyce again, and I hoped they would forgive me for disappearing like I had.

CHAPTER 10

The Future

OVER THE NEXT FEW days, I packed my case with all my very best, most beautiful clothes, and after making a trip to my hairdresser and purchasing myself some new make-up, I was ready to take Brutus to Joe and set off on my journey back to England.

I was in no hurry, so I enjoyed an overnight stay in a French hotel, which left me rested and relaxed as I headed for the Euro Tunnel and England. A few hours later, I was driving past the post office, where Joyce and I had worked together as friends and as business partners. Joyce had paid me for the shares I had in the post office some time ago.

I was shocked to see that the post office was no longer a post office. There were boxes of fruit and vegetables outside, and the shop window displayed food items and household items. It was no longer a post office but a village corner shop.

I parked up and slowly walked inside the little corner shop. I wondered if I would meet Joyce there, but by the look of the shopkeeper, I realised that Joyce must have sold up. I bought some flowers and chocolates, and I took a deep breath and asked the shopkeeper if Joyce was still involved with the former post office. The shopkeeper told me that he did not know of any Joyce, as he had purchased the store from a Bulgarian family, so Joyce must have been there before their time.

I returned to my car and sat there for a short time, trying to collect my thoughts. I was tempted to turn around and go back home, but I knew I had to see Ben and Joyce and deliver my paperwork.

I set off and slowly drove down the long country lane towards where my cottage used to be. Every turn and view on that country lane brought back memories from when I used to live there. They were good memories; even the memories of Brutus going missing were memories worth keeping.

I pulled up at the side of the road, and I could see no evidence that my cottage had ever been there. I got out of the car and walked towards the plot of land. I could see some of the stonework on the ground, covered with brambles and weeds. There was no evidence to show the remains of my lovely little cottage from my past, as it was completely overgrown.

As I stood there feeling quite bewildered, across the road, from the entrance of Formby Estate and House, two large cars drove out. The large doors behind them then closed tightly shut.

I remembered how I used to wait at the front of my cottage to get a glimpse of Professor Malcolm James McKenzie as he returned or left. I had been totally smitten by him. I had lived in hope that he would notice me and one day return my unrequited love. What a waste of time that had been! I had wasted so much of my life living in the hope that the love I had for Malcolm would be returned and that Malcolm and I would live happily ever after. What a fool I had been!

I returned to my car, and I sat there and cried. I cried for me. I cried for Malcolm. I cried for my burnt-out cottage. I cried for the hurt and anguish I must have caused Joyce and Ben.

It was quite a while before I could console myself. I was very upset. I started driving away, and I headed for the town. I was in no fit state to go and visit Ben's farm.

Feeling sick, upset, and tired, I booked myself into a small motel on the outskirts of the town.

After a long, hot soak in the bath, and after eating the complimentary biscuits and drinking a hot complimentary coffee in the room, I curled up and eventually fell asleep.

The next morning, I woke up with swollen eyes. I did not want to look so bad, but the weather was beautiful outside, so I took my time dressing and preparing for the day. I enjoyed a large breakfast at a small café near the motel, and after I had packed my case, I returned to my car.

I sat in my car for what seemed like ages. What was I to do? Was I to return home, or was I to be brave and full of confidence and go and visit Ben and Joyce? I wanted to just turn around and set back to France, but I had the papers for Ben, so I looked in the driving mirror to check that my eyes were not as swollen, and then I set off.

I drove down the long country lane towards the ruins of my cottage and then along the country road that led to Ben Wilcock's Farm. I could see the farmhouse in the distance, and my heart was pounding so much; I had given myself quite a headache.

As I reached the farmhouse, there were no cars or vehicles parked outside. I pulled up in front of the front door and then walked around to the back door. I knocked, but nobody answered.

I slowly walked towards the rear yard. I remembered Brutus being held in one of the barns after the cottage fire. I fought back the tears. The last thing I wanted was for my eyes to swell up again. I wanted to look good and confident, but there was no way I felt good and confident. I was a mess. I was breaking up inside.

I returned to my car yet again, and as I drove away, I noticed a very large, new industrial-type building further along the lane. I decided to drive further down the lane to see what the building was. A sign over the large gateway answered my question. It read, "Wilcock's Equestrian Centre and Horse Riding School". I drove in through the entrance and parked up.

I was feeling so proud of Ben. He worked so hard for his farm and his animals. He deserved everything he worked hard for.

The riding school building and the yard to the rear were hives of activity. The stable block to the side of the building was also very busy. I could see horses in many of the surrounding fields, and of course there were cows in many other fields.

I sat in my car, wondering what to do next. As a couple of women riders came through the internal perimeter gate, I walked over to them and asked them if they knew where I might find Mr. Ben Wilcock or Mrs. Joyce Wilcock. They told me they had no idea but said he was usually somewhere on the farm. I thanked them, and then I made my way into the large indoor riding area.

As I entered the riding area, I suddenly felt quite sick. I turned around and made my way back to my car. I drove back to the motel, where I booked another room for that night.

For a couple of hours, I had my head in the toilet bowl. I was physically sick. I then lay on the bed and fell fast asleep.

It was mid-afternoon when I woke up. After a cup of tea, I felt much better. I blamed my emotional upset for the sickness. So I decided to try again to contact Ben and Joyce.

I showered, changed my clothes, put my make-up on, and redid my hair. At least by then my eyes were no longer swollen. I looked more presentable. Feeling much better and quite confident because of the way I looked, I set off again towards Wilcock's Farm.

I drove into the car park at the front of the house and parked up. Again I walked to the back door and knocked, but again there was no answer. I walked into the rear farm yard, where I could see and hear a noisy commotion made by farm vehicles, diggers, and waggons in the centre of a field nearby.

I stood and watched as men drove the diggers and pumps were being used to pump out what looked like slurry, which was then sucked into tanks on the waggons.

It was then that I saw Ben—tall, handsome Ben. He was walking to and fro, shouting orders to his workforce. They were all knee-high in the slurry. I could smell it from where I was stood. As soon as I saw Ben Wilcock, my heart started pounding; I was feeling extremely nervous and excited.

I watched as the tanker waggons drove away with their dirty loads. The farm digger drove away, and then all was quiet. There was no sign of anyone.

I walked back to the farmhouse and knocked on the back door. No answer.

I walked slowly down to the equestrian centre in the hope that I might see Ben, but they were closing for the day, and the lights were being turned off and doors were being locked.

Feeling quite insecure by then, I walked slowly back to the farmhouse and again knocked on the back door. Again there was no answer.

I walked into the rear farmyard, and suddenly the large barn door opened, and out walked Ben.

He stood there looking right at me. My heart was pounding, and as I looked into his eyes, a feeling of love and sexual sensations came over me.

"What the fuck do you want?" said Ben. "Well hello to you too," I replied.

"Fuck off, Pauline. Crawl back to where you came from!" shouted Ben.

"I have brought you the signed contract for the plot of land. I thought I would bring it and see you and Joyce."

"Leave it on the table in the kitchen, and then fuck off!" said Ben, and then he turned and walked back into the barn and closed the door behind him.

I was not going to leave until I had sorted this bad mess out. I stood there in the yard waiting. It was ages before Ben came out of the barn again, this time with his two dogs.

"You still here? Just leave, Pauline. I have had a very bad day. I am hungry, tired, and covered in shit. I do not want to be bothered by you!"

"What time will Joyce be back? I just want to see her before I go."

"Why the hell should Joyce be coming back? She is married and lives at the other end of town!" shouted Ben as he walked through the gate and into the field with his two dogs.

As Ben disappeared out of sight with his dogs, I turned and went to the back door of the farmhouse. The door was not locked, so I entered into the kitchen and sat down at the table. My heart was still pounding. I thought, *So! Ben and Joyce are not married. I must find out where she is living. I need to see her while I am in this area. I must also find out if Ben is married or if he is in a serious relationship.*

I did not want to leave until I had seen Ben again. While I was waiting, I glanced around the kitchen and dining area. The whole room was neat, tidy, and clean. There was some sort of casserole dish warming in the oven.

It was obvious that Ben still employed a housekeeper.

Before long, Ben came through the back door and into the kitchen. What a mess he was. He was dripping from head to toe in some sort of slurry, and by the smell of him, I guessed that it was septic tank effluent.

"I have left the papers on the table here," I said, pointing to them. "Fine, you can go now," retorted Ben.

"I thought you and Joyce had married, as I saw your engagement announcement in the local paper." Ben did not answer me, so I continued.

"Are you married now, Ben?"

"No," I said quietly. "Are you in a serious relationship?" I asked. "Are you?" was Ben's reply.

"No." I said again.

"Neither am I. Pauline, I am tired, dirty, and hungry, and I can do without you being here making small talk."

While I had been asking him the questions, Ben had started to take off all his sodden clothing. As he took it off, he threw it into the washing machine. Eventually he was standing in front of me stark naked, with all the dirty slurry dripping from him. He turned to me, held his hands out and said, "Do you want to dance?"

"No thank you, not at the moment," I replied and I looked into his eyes and smiled. I had such a strong feeling of love and lust for Ben at that moment.

Ben ran out of the kitchen and up the stairs, presumably to bathe or shower. Before long, I could hear the water running in the shower.

I knew what I had to do. I slowly went up the stairs, and I gently pushed the bathroom door open. Ben was in the shower, and when he saw me, he handed me a large sponge.

"Try to get this shit off my back. I think it has gone solid, like concrete. Yes, I think it is shit concrete."

I told Ben to put some shower gel on the sponge, and then I cleaned Ben's back. Ben grabbed my wrist and pulled me into the shower, pushing me up against the side of the stall. His lips were pressing hard against mine, and his wet body was pushed up against me. As he let go of my wrist, I placed my arms around his neck and shoulders, and I pulled him more towards me. I had forgotten how good Ben used to make me feel. I had forgotten how good Ben felt.

We both laughed as we tried to remove my clothes, which were very wet by that time.

I could feel his penis pressing up against me. Then it was between my legs, and then I felt his penetration. It was not long before I climaxed, and then I felt Ben's ejaculation.

We held onto each other for quite a while. I could feel Ben's panting breath against my neck. I did not want to let him go, but soon he had grabbed a towel and left the bathroom. I continued to shower myself, and then I wrapped a towel around me. As I was leaving the bathroom, Ben was running downstairs, fully dressed.

"You will find some dry clothes in your old room," shouted Ben from the kitchen.

I entered the room I used to have, and I was surprised to see that it seemed to be just as I had left it all that time ago. Perfume and some jewellery were still on the dressing table and in the wardrobe, and some of my clothes were still there.

I quickly dressed, and then I made my way back downstairs to the kitchen. Ben had dished out two plates of hot food from the casserole dish I had seen in the oven.

Ben was busy eating his meal as he was reading over the papers I had brought. I sat down and started to eat. We did not speak to each other. I was aware of the atmosphere that was in that room. I was still feeling the aftermath of that wonderful sex we had had.

I eagerly watched Ben. He was a fine figure of a man. As we both sat there eating the hot food, we made no conversation. Every so often, we looked into each other's eyes. I knew I had a powerful feeling of love for Ben.

I heard the noise of a car pulling up outside. "Well, that's my lift.

Close the door when you leave," said Ben as he opened the back door.

"Wait, Ben! Please, will you marry me? I am still in love with you!" I shouted Ben stopped and hesitated, but he did not turn around to look at me.

Then he closed the door behind him, and I heard the car drive away.

I sat there and recalled how Ben had asked me to marry him more than once in the past. Each time, I refused. Then Ben lost his patience with me and told me he would never ask me to marry him again, ever. He said that if I ever wanted to change my mind and marry him, I would have to ask him. Well, I had just done that!

Before I left, I collected all my wet clothes, cleared the table, and mopped the floor to remove all the effluent. I searched around the dining area for Ben's phone number, and then I saw his invoice book. His invoice book had his farm and equestrian centre details and, of course, the farm's telephone number, email address, and Ben's mobile number. I drove back to the motel, made myself a hot drink, and sat on the bed, wondering what to do next.

With the information I had found in the kitchen at the farm, I decided to text Ben: "You once told me that you would never ask me to marry you again, ever, and that if I changed my mind and wanted to marry you, I would have to ask you to marry me. Well, I did just that tonight. When I saw you today, I realised that I loved you, and I proved that tonight as well. I need an answer. Mr. Wilcock, will you marry me?"

I did not need to put my name to the text; he would know who it was from. All I had to do was wait for a reply. That reply never came!

The following day, I took my time having a breakfast, and as I had not received a reply from Ben by the time I finished, I set off on my journey home to France.

I took my time driving home. I even made an overnight stop in northern France. I constantly checked my phone, hoping and praying that Ben would answer me. I needed a yes or a no. He never replied. I could tell by the way he had made love to me in his shower that he still wanted me, so I continued to wait for his answer.

I arrived home safe, and after collecting Brutus, I carried on with my daily routine in France. I had always been content with my life—especially in France. But since my most recent visit to Wilcock Farm, my thoughts were always of Ben Wilcock. Some nights I would wake up with a start, remembering the passion and the sex Ben and I had shared in the shower that evening. I thought surely Ben must have some feelings for me.

I tried telephoning the farm, but there was only an answering machine. I did not want to talk to a machine. I tried Ben's mobile, but he never answered it, and it always seem to go to voicemail.

With the email address I had for Wilcock Farm, I decided to try, one more time, to contact Ben.

I wrote a simple email: "Please contact me . . . Pauline." And then I wrote my mobile number down.

Still he did not contact me. My fretting and upset feelings, soon turned to anger. How dare he ignore me? Just a yes or no was all I wanted, but instead I was waiting and waiting for a reply from Ben Wilcock.

I needed an answer. I needed some closure. Again I took Brutus to Joe's, and I told Joe that I just needed a week or so away. I was so grateful to Joe. He was a wonderful friend.

Once again, I packed a case and started another journey to England. I needed to confront Ben. I could not carry on pining for Ben. I knew that I really loved him, and I knew that there was a very good chance that he still loved me in return. Life was too short to mess about waiting for someone. I had been chasing love and happiness all my life, and it had to stop. I was going to make a stand for my sanity.

During that journey, I decided not to stop overnight on the way to England. I drove straight to the motel I usually stayed at. I collapsed in the room and slept until the following day.

That morning, feeling rested and refreshed, I prepared myself for a visit to see Ben. I wore my best outfit, and I made myself look as good as I could.

"Could you tell me if Ben Wilcock is here?" I asked politely.

"Sorry, no. He is at the livestock auctions today," the woman replied. "All right, I will call again. Thanks."

As I turned to walk away, the woman said, "Are you Pauline?" "Yes, I am."

"Ben has left you an envelope for me to give to you if you called," said the woman, who was obviously Ben's housekeeper.

I waited near my car until the woman brought me the envelope from Ben.

I sat in my car, just looking at the white envelope. My heart was pounding, my hands were clammy, and I was feeling quite sick. I slowly opened it and took out the papers. The first thing I saw was a Post-it note on which was written, "LOVE YOU". I quickly tried to read what the other papers were. They were two marriage notice forms—one in the name of Ben Wilcock and the other in my name. The forms listed the relevant documents required, declarations, and fees. Ben's form had been fully completed.

Why had Ben not contacted me? I was angry, happy, confused, and very emotional. I sat in my car, looking at the Post-it note with the words "LOVE YOU" written on it, and I just burst into tears. I was an emotional wreck.

When I had composed myself, I phoned Ben's mobile. That time, he answered.

"Mr. Wilcock, at the moment, I am at the farm," I said before Ben interrupted me.

"Ah! So you have my envelope!"

"Why did you not contact me? I have been waiting every day for your phone call!"

"Pauline, I needed to be absolutely sure that you did indeed want to marry me. I thought that if I waited long enough, if you really wanted me, you would turn up at the farm again. Then I would be sure!"

"What if I had just given up on us and I had never returned to the farm looking for you?" I asked.

"Don't you worry! If, after a certain length of time, you had not been to see me, I would most certainly have come looking for you." He burst out laughing.

"So are we really going to do this? Are we really going to marry?" I asked.

"Yes and yes." Ben laughed as he continued speaking. "I love you, Pauline. I have missed you. Will you wait at the farm until I get home? Will you be in my bed tonight? Are you going to move back in with me?" asked Ben.

"Yes, yes, and yes!" I shouted excitedly.

Have a look at the form I have filled in, and see if there is anything else you you want from me.

"Ben, there is something I want from you," I said. "What is that?" replied Ben.

"I want from you a ring of love!

* 9 7 9 8 3 3 0 3 5 6 0 5 8 *